The Last Biome

and the Five Clades

The Last Biome and the Five Clades
Copyright © 2014 by Hazel Espinar. All rights reserved.
Published by Six Pine Alley, LLC

Library of Congress Catalog Card Number 2014904943
ISBN 978-0-9960021-0-3 (pbk)
ISBN 978-0-9960021-1-0 (e-book)

Illustrated by Lawrence D. Colburn
Edited by Jeff Fleischer

First Edition
Printed in the United States of America

Visit us at www.lastbiome.com

ACKNOWLEDGEMENTS

My parents, sister and

Charlie, an old friend

CONTENTS

CHAPTER ONE

ECO-JAR FINDS

At the end of a long cul-de-sac, nestled in the beautiful, abundant prairie grasses in the town of Barrenville, sat a thinly constructed, rectangular, ranch-style home. The home had high, sloped ceilings and moderately sized rooms. Unlike the rest of the facade, the back of the home had floor-to-ceiling windows, offering a clear view of the long backyard, and the forest in the near distance.

The ranch was part of a residential community called Sumberlakes, one of three distinct communities within Barrenville. The Sumberlakes development consisted of medium-sized, single-family homes. The other two communities were called Old Town and Lapiz. Old Town had three-story row houses, while the numerous private estates of Lapiz sat atop rolling hills. The Lapiz development was the farthest south, followed by Sumberlakes, with Old Town the farthest north. Barrenville also had a commercial tract just north of its residential communities, which included the town's shops, schools, post office, library, museum, and other public buildings. The buildings within the commercial tract formed a spiral-shaped design, with the buildings closest to the core clustered more tightly together than the buildings farther away.

A stretch of the prairie path extended mainly north and south along the eastern outskirts of Barrenville's residential communities and commercial tract. The manmade path through the forest ran sixty-one miles, longer than some countries. Aside from the area's wildlife, only pedestrians, bicycles, and the occasional baby stroller or pogo stick had traveled down the limestone prairie path. Like waves hitting the shore and resurfacing the shoreline, the virgin prairie was stapled by railroad tracks, then altered again for hiking purposes.

East of the Lapiz community and the path, bookended by Lake Michigan, was an area called Settlers' Hills, which took up a stretch of land as vast and long as the rest of Barrenville combined. Settlers' Hills had an extensive farm, a laboratory facility known as Mera Lab, a private school called Mera Academy, and an underground energy generator. Trees sparsely covered the north and northwest sectors of Settlers' Hills leading to the forest beyond. The southernmost sector contained Hoise

Farm, tucked between extensive crop-production domes to the east and immediate north, and Mera Lab and the adjacent Mera Academy to the west. From Settlers' Hills, Lake Michigan appeared as vast as an ocean. A colossal car dealership sat west of Barrenville's landscape, an indicator of the greater commercial traffic ahead in the next city. Barrenville's remaining border contained a sparse forest buffering the outskirts of the city of Chicago to the south.

The Sepvans—Ansel, an engineer; Hady, a stay-at-home mom; and their children, twelve-year-old Peet and six-year-old Marilyn—lived in the ranch house at the end of the cul-de-sac. Peet, a lanky and curious fellow, had an uninhibited passion and unmatched curiosity for life. Peet's favorite pastime was finding the rare grass clearings or barren spots in the palpably rich, black, wet, sand-textured soil of Barrenville's unruly prairie grasses and nearby forest. From those spots he would collect specimens of plant remnants, dirt, rocks, and an occasional insect, and assemble what he called "eco-jars." He labeled each jar according to specific destinations on the grid-lined chart of Barrenville he always carried with him during such adventures.

One late afternoon, as the sun began to set below the horizon, Peet sat at the picnic table in his backyard, puncturing holes in the lids of new jars. Out of the corner of his eye, he spotted a large, upright, white frog. In one long leap, the frog flew across the yard, and seamlessly slipped under the cement gutter guard along the house. It was a most unusual sight, which prompted Peet to run in the direction of the gutter. As he approached, he scratched his head in wonder. He had never seen such an oddly shaped and strangely colored frog before, nor an upright frog with acrobatic skill. Nor could he explain how such a large creature could squeeze so quickly and effortlessly under such a small guard. Determined to see the frog again, he knelt down to run his fingers along the gutter, looking for a pocket where he could insert his fingers to lift the heavy gutter guard, but couldn't find an opening. There were two inches of dirt between the guard and the grass. Fearing the frog underneath might suffocate, he eagerly scraped the dirt away from the gutter with his fingertips until he removed enough that he could grip one side of the heavy gutter.

As Peet lifted the end of the gutter, more sunlight pierced the unusually deep cavity in the ground, causing the far-away frog within to crouch lower. When the sun's rays reached the back of the guard and flooded the entire cavity, the frog opened its eyes. Peet immediately noticed the eyes were almond shaped and flashed like emeralds. The distinctive frog had three overlapping sacs on each side of its spine, like multiple bags slung over a donkey. It also had a spiny lower back. Peet was taken aback by the frog's sharp and unusual color, and its almost statuesque appearance. Just then, Hady called him into the house. Startled, Peet turned away to respond and, when he looked back, the frog had disappeared. Peet placed his arm into the now-empty cavity, and felt only cool, wet soil. No tunnels or crevices stemmed from the cavity.

"Where did this creature come from?" Peet wondered. He

also wondered what it meant that this frog was so oddly shaped, and chalk white instead of a normal green or brown. During dinner, Peet made no mention of this creature, which he had fondly named Jinko.

During recess at school the next day, Peet rounded up Marilyn and his classmates Ray and Jill, to tell them all about his encounter with Jinko. Marilyn had big, light-brown eyes, lashes that could swat a dragonfly clear across the room, and chestnut hair always molded into two high pigtails with the ends nearly touching the middle of her back. She wore the standard navy-blue-and-white school uniform, but embedded rainbow-colored ribbons in her pigtails, and used the same strands as shoelaces to add color to her bulky, white, uniform shoes. Marilyn was playful, highly energetic, and adored all kinds of creatures—especially those predisposed to flee from her, as her instinct was to embrace those she could catch.

"We can dig a pond in our backyard so he'll have a home," Marilyn said, when Peet told them about the frog. She envisioned placing her doll-sized summer clubhouse—complete with swimming pool, grill, and attached Jacuzzi—alongside the pond to serve as scenery. Peet nodded in agreement.

Ray was a lean athlete of average height, and had a robust charm. He had strawberry-colored hair, piercing green eyes, a strong jawline, and a face speckled by a combination of freckles and light acne. Ray recalled learning in school that amphibians, and frogs in particular, served as health indicators of their habitat.

"Peet, maybe this frog is white because it is ill," Ray said.

"All white? No colors at all?" Marilyn interjected. All the kids giggled, knowing how Marilyn liked to splash an empty white canvas with an explosive array of colors.

"I don't think the frog is ill, because he could move really quickly through the grasses," Peet said. "And besides, his eyes were bright green, and they sparkled."

Jill, who had shoulder-length, blonde hair and light-brown eyes, was the tallest in their class and had a no-nonsense, practical approach to life. "Hmmm...you probably saw Jinko close to dusk because his skin is pale and sensitive to the sun," she said.

"Okay, then he can swim at night so his skin won't burn," Ray said.

"Over the weekend I'll look for a good spot in our backyard for the pond," Peet responded. Marilyn smiled. "The pond should draw him out, and the reflection of the moon hitting the water might just give him enough light exposure to change color," Peet continued.

Marilyn, who was now struggling to tilt her head upward, exclaimed, "Jinko is a moon frog!" They all chuckled, noting how long she had been standing in the center of the group, looking up at them with her long, hanging pigtails.

"Do you really think that natural moonlight will give Jinko a normal frog color?" Jill asked.

"Possibly, but it's best we do it on a full moon," Ray said. "This way, he'll get the maximum amount of moonlight."

"We also don't want to leave the land dug up any longer than necessary," Jill said. "I'll help pull out the roots so we can replant them later."

They all agreed it was an ingenious plan, but they would have to learn when the next full moon would occur before they started to dig. The group disbursed like marbles tossed over a slanted plane, reaching the school doors in the order of their running abilities. Yet, before they could begin their search for a calendar, recess had ended. School monitors interrupted their plan and rerouted the children back to their classes.

*   *   *

Barrenville's school district consisted of two public schools and one private school. From first grade through eighth grade, students attended a primary school called Fareens, before going to the public high school. After high school, most of Barrenville's kids left the small town for college—unless they were among the few students admitted to Mera Academy. It was a universally known, and widely acclaimed, private institution teaching international students from first grade through college. Mera Academy's entrance criteria were never published, and no one outside of the admissions department seemed to know how children were selected to attend the school. Money, ethnicity, language skills, sports skills, fame, power—none were sufficient leverage to catapult a child into the institution. Mera Academy produced only extraordinary leaders for their industries and communities.

In addition to the unique school system, Barrenville had unprecedented laws to preserve the integrity of its land, with strict laws against excavating within the town limits. The laws focused on the native grass roots, which influenced the overall complex root system—including a mix of naturally occurring native roots and hybrid roots developed in Settlers' Hills. In fact, anyone who sought to disrupt the native prairie grass roots required both a "peg" permit and the services of a "Clamper," a worker from Settlers' Hills who surveyed the land prior to excavation and, in most cases, performed the authorized digging.

At an early age, Barrenville children were taught about preservation and conservation, and how to co-exist with the town's various grasses. Play zones were marked along each of the schools and residential communities, so children could gather and play freely within those areas. Barrenville dwellers understood and respected that they were living above the largest remaining native prairie root metropolis left on Earth.

CHAPTER TWO

UPROOTING THE NATIVES

On Saturday morning, Peet slipped into the loafers his father kept near the patio door and walked outside to survey the backyard. As Peet stood on the patio overlooking the backyard, he became overwhelmed with the nuances, intricacies, colors, and textures of this special land. The yard was well texturized, with grasses of various heights. As his eyes focused in on a more granular level, he noticed that dew coated each blade of grass and the petals of each wildflower. In the distance, he observed two grand monarch butterflies settled on the milkweeds, where caterpillars were nestling and eating through the leaves. A pair of rabbits ate ferociously while watching Peet cautiously from a distance. The prairie was charged with life, and the air had a memorable quality that morning. All was calm and peaceful.

Peet, whose fingertips were in regular contact with the ground from all his eco-jar collecting, felt confident that no one would notice if he dug just a small hole in the ground for a pond. A surge of cautious excitement came over him. The feeling quickly dissipated, however, when he thought of his father's warnings not to play on the native grasses. Ansel frequently reminded Peet and Marilyn that they had designated play zones all throughout the town, so there was no need to disturb the grasses in the yard just for play.

Marilyn turned on the television, intending to watch her Saturday morning cartoons, and blared the volume so loudly Peet could faintly hear it from the backyard. He spotted Marilyn running between the living room and adjacent kitchen, both of which faced the backyard. As he walked through the yard, Peet became entranced by the hope of finding a barren pocket of land, the same way he skillfully had for years when collecting specimens for eco-jars in other parts of town. After searching for some time and finding none, Peet selected a spot in the farthest northeast corner of the backyard, hidden directly behind a row of green shrubbery.

Peet knelt down on the grass in a crawl position and pushed down further into the ground, molding pressure points with his knees and hands. As he clenched his hands around the bunches of grass, he took pause, remembering he didn't have permission to dig in his backyard. But how else was he going to build the pond? Anyway, his friends had planned to help, and he thought they'd appreciate him getting a head start.

His body was now stretched out along the grass, with the sun's rays soothing his back and exposed neck. While he pondered his actions, a large, black water beetle violently struck him in the right eye. Startled, he immediately released the grasses from his hands and darted inside, barely able to see. Peet opened the patio door and quietly stepped into the kitchen behind his mother, who was adding brightly colored vegetables to the scrambled eggs. "Wash up for breakfast, Peet," Hady said.

In the bathroom, Peet repeatedly washed out his eyes. The overwhelming pain from the injury to his right eye was now irritating his left eye as well. For a moment, he thought he was going blind and that nature was punishing him for trying to rip the grasses out of the ground. When he stopped rubbing his eyes and opened them, he saw silver droplets floating in the air in many directions. He rubbed his eyes again. When he looked down at the bathroom's tile floor, the specks and spots on the tile appeared to cluster and form shapes of different objects, with a silver lining around each. When he raised his eyes to gaze at the decoratively spotted bathroom curtains, he saw the shapes of more objects with the same linings. He again bent down in front of the sink, cupped more lukewarm water into his hands, and splashed his eyes until his vision was completely restored. When he saw his reflection in the mirror above the sink, his injured eye was red, and both eyes had swollen slightly.

As he walked down the hallway and back into the kitchen,

Peet heard chaotic sounds that reminded him of the school cafeteria. He tried to compose himself, as the last thing he wanted was to be interrogated about how he had been struck in the eye. Then it dawned on him—a water beetle? He hadn't even scraped the dirt, let alone filled a pond with water, so how could he have attracted a water beetle from the lake a couple of miles away?

He turned the corner into the kitchen, nearly tripping over his sister. Marilyn was sitting on her knees in front of the pantry, where she kept an extensive collection of cereal boxes that she used to create a makeshift fortress around herself during meals. "Which cereal boxes should I use today?" she asked herself. The boxes varied in size, as well as in the art and games on the back. Marilyn frequently built her fortress by placing the boxes on each side of her place at the table, to keep her eyes shielded from ketchup, mustard, and anything else she found distasteful. Peet grabbed a plate from the counter and stood in the family buffet line behind his dad, who was scooping portions of food from each of the platters spread across the counter. As Marilyn placed the scattered boxes back on the shelves, she noticed Peet had large, green stains on the knees of his pajama pants. "Of course!" Marilyn said quietly. She immediately guessed he had started work on Jinko's pond. Worse, he had started without her.

Peet took a heaping spoonful of perfectly textured, creamy scrambled eggs with vegetables, and loaded it up next to the mixed fruit and sausage on his plate. Marilyn lined up next, and piled the fluffy blueberry pancakes on her plate. At the table, she skillfully removed the blueberries from the cakes, just as she always removed peas from rice. She even removed the "O" shapes from her cereal by crushing each piece in her little fingers, then placing the residue in her spoonful of milk. No one in the family flinched at either her eating habits or her custom fortresses; they only noted the oddity of it all when guests pointed it out. Hady finally sat down after bringing a handful of napkins and a saltshaker to the table. The family discussed the menu for their routine Saturday family barbeque. Marilyn, however, sat quietly at the table that morning, entertaining herself within the fortress. She decided Peet was as distasteful as the ketchup he used for his eggs.

Near the end of breakfast, Ansel announced that he and Peet were traveling to Wisconsin in search of his favorite, hard-to-find wood for the barbeque that evening. Hady knew her husband, a car fanatic, also enjoyed taking casual, long road trips. Ansel took great pride in grilling meats to everyone's taste using the blazing inferno created from his custom-made grill. Ansel and his brother-in-law Fred had jointly drawn up the blueprints and built the grill structure next to the patio, a grill the family affectionately called the "The Ansel." He practiced the Argentinean grilling techniques he learned from his father in Buenos Aires, dousing the logs with oils and injecting spice blends into the meats hours prior to cooking. The entire neighborhood could count on Ansel to provide a gut-awakening aroma, piped through the grill's elongated chimney, nearly every weekend. Peet, remembering his nearly untouched pond project, began to complain about having to travel. His mother gently pressed her hand on Peet's shoulder as she got up to get more coffee, and suggested he accompany his father on the long-distance road trip so Ansel wouldn't have to travel alone. Peet reluctantly agreed.

After Peet and Ansel left home, Marilyn headed into the backyard to begin probing for signs of digging. As if by instinct, Marilyn was drawn to the same spot that Peet had already marked behind the shrubs. She saw the four indentations in the grass where Peet had crouched down. Like Peet, Marilyn knew that puncturing the ground, uprooting or severing any of the native grasses in the yard, was absolutely prohibited. Her hands trembled, but she could not resist. She rationalized that the pond would help a feeble Jinko survive, and the vitamins from the rays of the moonlight would re-energize him and give him back his color.

Marilyn thought she'd surprise Peet when he returned home by getting a good start on the pond project. She returned several times to the shed to gather tools, including an old barrel ring, craft scissors, her mom's trowel, and her industrial-size boxes of colored clays. Hady, who had stepped on the patio to check on Marilyn, observed her leaving the shed with her clays. Hady turned back into the house, pleased Marilyn could entertain herself so well. After Hady closed the patio door, Marilyn tucked away behind the shrubbery and placed her barrel ring over the four indentations, making an outline for the pond. Next, she used the craft scissors to trim the grass around the ring, so she could see which grasses to pull, while keeping the circle shape. She also used the trowel to loosen the bundled grass roots.

Once it became obvious exactly which grasses to pull for the pond, she knelt down and tightly bundled the tall grasses within the circle. She clenched as many blades of grass in each hand as she could, knowing that the roots down in the ground were even taller than her. While falling back and using her body weight to pull, she met an unexpected resistance from the strong net of native prairie grass roots. Now with the roots partially exposed, she stood up, swept up the grasses, and hugged them with her forearms across her chest. The unearthing of the grasses was for Jinko, she reminded herself. She closed her eyes and gave one last tug with all her might. The roots' ends snapped and popped as they were torn out of the ground. Grasses with thick, plum-colored roots dangled from her hands and arms. All that remained was a gaping hole that appeared to lead to a distant chamber below.

Oddly, unknotting the layer of sod from the earth felt somehow familiar to Marilyn, like pulling out stubborn flesh and seeds from a pumpkin. Suddenly, a brief gust of wind came from the chamber, pushing Marilyn atop the small mound of pulled grass she had just laid behind her. A foreign, sweet scent infused the air in every direction within at least ten yards of the chamber. Her senses became overstimulated, and she stood there in a daze. When her senses returned, she realized she had yet to mold the clay for the pond; first, however, she would have to stash the grasses. She placed all the unearthed roots into a large, black garbage bag, and rolled them up as if wrapping sushi. She then worked laboriously to mix the clays together, and molded the clay into the shape of a sink basin, big enough to snugly fit the hole. Once the clay hardened, she thought, the pond would be ready for water. Proud of her work, Marilyn returned inside.

It was shortly after dusk when Peet and Ansel finally arrived home, both carrying several logs under each arm. It was dark when the family finally sat down to have their always-memorable Saturday barbeque dinner. Peet had decided on his way home from the trip to retouch the grasses he had disheveled the next morning.

That night, the Earth—as an organism made of water, continents, gases, plants, and creatures— created a sound heard only by wildlife. Mammals, birds, and sea life were restless that night, as they heard the distant cry of the native prairie root metropolis, now punctured and torn. A painful wound had opened in Barrenville.

CHAPTER THREE

THE GENETS AND
THE WHIMSICAL TREE

Sunday morning, after the long road trip with his father, followed by unusually restless sleep, Peet decided to hit the prairie path for some weekend exploration and specimen gathering. During his longer-than-usual trek, this time veering off the beaten path, he discovered a long, perfect row of leafless trees. Their dangling limbs and branches so thickly intertwined that they blocked most views of the landscape beyond. This thicket of intertwined branches sharply contrasted with the rest of the forest, as if it was intentionally hiding something beyond. Peet grew more curious as he struggled to pass through the thicket.

Eventually, he stepped into a serene clearing in the shape of a half-circle, enclosed by trees on the remaining sides and a protruding cliff ahead. Just beyond that cliff, he could see branches in the shape of a mushroom cap. Peet walked toward the cliff's edge and, once there, noticed a second plateau below that also protruded out over the lake.

This plateau held a most unusual specimen—a spiral-shaped tree surrounded by white sand and blue shrubs. The shrubbery left blue specks in the white sand, with the sand closest to the shrubs speckled heaviest. This was the strangest tree Peet had ever seen. Its thickly braided trunk was a dark, rich, caramel color, with patches of what appeared to be fur along its base. The tree's branches stretched as high as the cliff above, in all directions.

Peet peered out into the lake and observed two separate bodies of waters. The inside waters, immediately surrounding the double cliffs, had an unusual ebb-and-flow pattern that kept the same velocity and rhythm whether moving toward or away from the cliff. The movement of these waves was similar to that of carrying a basin of water across a room in slow motion, except each wave spouted a crest of white foam. Also, the belly of each of wave glistened sterling silver with a unique fish-scale pattern, while its outside matched the rest of the waters. The combined motion of the two bodies of water was captivating and soothing, and the sounds emanating from the lake were softer closer to the double cliffs. Also, a circle of thickly layered white clouds hung directly over the spiraled tree, like an umbrella top protecting the stem directly beneath it.

Peet next focused his attention on the Whimsical Tree itself—its texture, colors, and unusual shape. Along the trunk, Peet noticed what appeared to be the side of a doorframe. Using the branches closest to the cliff's edge, he climbed his way down the tree and onto the doorstep. At his shoulder level, Peet found a tiny sign that read, "Genets." Before he could knock, a pale, slender man almost Peet's height opened the door. He had slanted, black eyes with thick, black-framed glasses. The man wore an elegant, white dress robe with layered lapels and double tails.

"Come in, friend," the man stated as he further opened the door. "My name is Jacq." Peet waited to enter until he could fully view the curiously inviting entranceway. There was an aromatic, wafting warmth about it. "I knew we would have a guest for tea any moment now. It is ready," Jacq said, half to himself and half to Peet. Jacq led him past the entranceway and into the grand parlor without another word. The inside of the tree was startlingly different from the outside. Its interior walls were completely lined with white brick, and the floor was wooden. In the parlor, an immense crystal chandelier hung above six petite, white tables, some round and others square. Each had a plank tabletop partially covered by white-linen runners, and a bent-glass cylinder filled with white roses. Two white, wooden chairs at each table completed the setting. The whole parlor had a tranquil feel that Peet knew he would always remember. Along the interior of the parlor were offshoot branches with visible corridors at various heights, each leading to different-sized, hollowed rooms. Above each corridor hung a tiny sign identifying the rooms, including the three private rooms labeled "Jacq," "David," and "Sal."

While Peet settled into one of the chairs, Jacq called out to his two brothers in their private rooms, using a remote-control plane that shot hard candies at their doors. From their private rooms, the two brothers dropped into the parlor using rope ladders. Peet observed how the three were very similar in appearance, with the exceptions of their dispositions and heights. He was amused by how the three of them moved around the parlor. Peet felt oddly at ease, but famished at the same time. Just as Peet's stomach grumbled loudly, Jacq presented a plank tray with an appetizing spread of finger foods, pastries, apple juice, and tea to accompany the conversation.

"What do you call yourself?" Jacq inquired.

"Peet." He then asked them, collectively and politely, "Who are you?"

"We are called Genets," Jacq responded, "and we have been assigned as guardians of this Whimsical Tree and its crystallized, magical bone roots."

"Magical bone roots?" Peet repeated, startled.

"Yes," David said. "You see, long ago, the last Regal Deer stood atop this very cliff. The deer was as large as a prehistoric mammoth. It held one of the highest orders of respect in the animal kingdom due to its sheer size, stature, and strength, and it was also highly evolved.

"One day, a woman traversing the forest saw a hunter take aim at this majestic deer as it stood on this very cliff, overlooking the waters below. As the hunter positioned himself to shoot, the woman uncloaked herself, revealing she was a powerful being—the Cone Witch. She cast a spell on the Regal Deer and transformed it into this spiral tree we guard today. The deer's antlers are now the roots of this tree, and its body is integrated into the fibers of the bark.

"The Witch had the power to encapsulate living creatures and turn them into barren trees. The Regal Deer has survived as this living tree only because it had a more potent, uncontrollable magical energy than any being she'd encapsulated before, an energy we call Juso. It even took on this most unusual tree form, allowing us to protect it until someday it could break free. Over time, however, its weight caused the edge of the cliff to sink halfway to the waters below.

"Regal Deer were always rare, even when the continent was covered by millions of acres of grasses," David continued. "The Regal Deer and the grasslands were interdependent, needing each other to thrive. For thousands of years, these deer would sweep the fields with their antlers as they roamed the vast prairies, breaking up the concentrated bundles of roots that formed near the surface because of an overcrowding of roots. Their magical antlers also organically repaired tangles and healed tears in the fields. They were a natural and necessary part of the prairie grass environment."

"You cannot overwhelm the boy with all these ancient stories in one sitting," Jacq said, before turning to Peet. "How is our friend Wanerhess Hoise? It's been ages since we last saw him."

The question about Wanerhess burst the building tension

Peet felt, with needlepoint precision. Peet was happy for the break from the story and to know that the Genets also knew Wanerhess. A farmer, educator, and inventor, Wanerhess was well known in Barrenville as the Council-appointed caretaker of Settlers' Hills. "My family frequently visits Hoise Farm to buy goods. Wanerhess appeared to be well the last time I saw him," Peet said, finishing up his snack. Peet was relaxed again, and an acutely sensitive Jacq noticed.

"There's more, Peet, but we'll have to go outside to show you," David said, nodding at the others. He placed his napkin on the table and Peet followed in queue, with Sal and Jacq shuffling behind.

As they stood near the base of the tree, Sal knelt down by the exposed tree roots and placed his hands on the roots with great care. Peet next heard a snap on the ground. Sal stood up and presented Peet with a wooden chisel of unusual detail.

"Peet, unlike other antler marrow, this chisel contains living marrow mass, and it is magical," Sal said. Peet noted that Sal was far more dramatic than Jacq or David, both in his facial expressions and in his wispy voice. "Your destiny calls on you to be a part of this Regal Deer's legacy."

Peet thanked them as he examined the chisel with curiosity and confusion.

"As the grasslands became smaller and fragmented, the species of animals connected to them also became rarer," Sal said. "Most species, driven to cluster sizes on these few continents, will generally disappear over time. Now all but this last Regal Deer on the cliff are extinct. The branches continue to grow through the creature's strength and willingness to live. We hope this encapsulated life will one day again use its power to repair and heal the torn and dismembered grasslands."

Saddened by the story about the Regal Deer, Peet placed the chisel in his pocket and turned to observe the lake. When he looked back to where the three Genets were standing, they were already at the doorway waving goodbye. Peet hiked up to the higher cliff and walked in the direction from which he came. While traveling back home on the prairie path, he felt the land pulsate beneath his feet. When he exited the forest, the bouncing grasses propelled him in the direction of home at a pace he'd never known before. The view of the sun smudging in the horizon, and the words of the three Genets, echoed in his mind. He realized he had arrived home only when he grasped the porch rail, with little memory of how he got there.

Peet stumbled through the front door, breathing as heavily as if he had run a marathon. He paced across the living room for a while until he could breathe more normally, then joined his parents in the family room. Ansel was sitting in his usual recliner near the fireplace, reading the newspaper. Hady, who was organizing random items on the coffee table, observed that Peet looked pale and disheveled.

"Are you alright?" she asked worriedly.

Before Peet could answer, Ansel lowered his newspaper and interrupted. "Why do you do this to yourself?" Ansel asked excitedly. "You need to limit your outdoor activities because of your asthma and find a new hobby instead of those eco-jars."

"I need to know," Peet said in a soft voice. "I need to know about Barrenville's history and how the town came to be this way." In school, the children were taught about what was prohibited, with an emphasis on conservation, but there was no mention of why Barrenville was created atop America's largest prairie.

"Why right now, Peet, in this condition you are in? Where have you been?" Ansel asked now calmly, carefully observing Peet's body language.

"Please, Dad," Peet said. He settled into the sofa closest to his father.

While Peet had been on his prairie-path journey, Marilyn was busy laying out her dollhouse estate near the pond. The estate included a pool with an attached Jacuzzi, a café with patio furniture, and a golf cart—all of which she used to accessorize her newly constructed pond. Marilyn worked on the architecture of the pond's new landscape while propped up on her favorite multi-colored quilt, which she had jumbled up as a cushion beneath her. When she finished, she stood up to observe her accomplishment. A gentle breeze came across the land, caressing her whole body, assuring her that Peet would be delighted to see the complete pond and surrounding doll-size structures. The weather that afternoon was as warm as a typical late spring day in the Midwest, and the sky was laced with a string of unusually fast-moving clouds. In view of her accomplishments, how could the caressing breeze mean anything else?

CHAPTER FOUR

BARRENVILLE'S HISTORY

Ansel removed his glasses, set his newspaper down beside him on the floor, and reclined back in his chair. "I'll tell you the story of Barrenville," he began.

"Once there was a thriving community of prairie grasses covering millions of acres, nearly all of what would become forty-three of the United States. As settlers churned small communities into ever-expanding cities, that huge prairie got broken up and all but eliminated. Just in the last two hundred years—because of farming, urban sprawl, and other development—what's left of that huge prairie is now just fragmented patches scattered across the continent.

"With the native prairie dwindling, and greater distances between the patches, the prairie root network also weakened. Outside of these isolated patches, the rest of the land was stripped of its rich topsoil, which is why we now have a predominately clay continent. With less than five percent of prairie lands remaining, the Council brought together some of the best teachers and scientists in the world. They intervened and set out to salvage and preserve as much living native prairie as possible.

"Is Barrenville one of those fragments?" Peet asked. "We have a lot of prairie grasses here."

"Yes, exactly," Ansel replied. "Barrenville is important because we have the largest concentration of native grasses left, and we're right in the center of the land the full prairie once covered. The prairie is a root society. That's why the Council chose to set up Mera Lab and its other operations here. The Council members are the principal architects of the town's infrastructure. The Council also bought up every available patch of prairie in the country. After the federal government, it is the second-largest owner of the remaining major prairie patches left in the country. All the prairie land that was not already preserved by government or tarnished by private landowners was preserved by the Council.

"The Council worked tirelessly to understand the effects of the disappearance of the prairies, and found the grasses naturally contained and stabilized the land. They determined if the native prairie continued to shrink, the weight and elasticity of its root netting wouldn't be able to retain the delicate balance between water and soil. The network of prairie roots bonds the continent together and prevents things like flooding and erosion. This root network also expands and contracts in response to changes, whether caused by Mother Nature or mankind. Above ground, the prairie grasses house an amazing diversity of plant and animal species. Breaking the land isolated plant and animal communities and diminished most of that diversity. Even more importantly, the Council knew that a certain amount of prairie-root netting was crucial for saving the grassland biome."

"What's a biome?" Peet asked.

"Good question. It's a life community of vegetation and animals connected to a large geographic area. Aquatic environments, tundra, forests, deserts, and grasslands, are all kinds of biomes. Think of taking a cookie cutter to fit any of these massive regions on the globe. Everything inside it, below and above, is connected to that type of biome. All the world's biomes are connected and co-exist together. Anything that damages one affects the others."

"Is that why Barrenville produces hybrids, to stabilize the land?"

"Right. The Council realized they would have to rebuild the prairies to also help balance the biomes. Where there used to be an unbroken sea of prairie, now it was more like a lot of islands, and they needed a way to reconnect them. So the Council developed a hybrid grass that easily blends together with our native grasses and mimics the root system of the natural grassland. The hybrids are shorter, but heavier, more resilient, and more elastic. Because those qualities make it the best sod available, the Council has been able to export the hybrid grasses all across the country. As the hybrids flourished, they've interlocked with the remaining native roots, and connected the islands—like joining pieces of a puzzle together to form an image. As more of the hybrids produced here in Settlers' Hills grew around the country, they also strengthened our Barrenville root metropolis and its pulsating dual-heart valves—the inner workings between our native and hybrid roots."

"But how do they grow the hybrids? Is that what the domes are for, Dad?"

"The Council took advantage of our natural landscape to preserve the heart of the prairies through organic methods, like the domes in Settlers' Hills. The domes hold a massive crop of hybrids, using a vertical farming technique, and they occupy most of the land in Settlers' Hills. The dome design took advantage of the town's natural landscape formed mounds near the lake. The domes are laid out in near-perfect rows, and look like honeycombs split in half. They have aeration holes and pocket slips, which hold the growing native grasses in bundles. Outside the slips, the roots of the hybrid seedlings lay just beneath the surface, like a heavy moss. The hybrid roots grow horizontally and weave themselves into a fibrous tangle, and that unusual pattern resulted in what technicians from Mera Lab called "root mesh." Once the root mesh is produced, the harvesting equipment pulls the root mesh at a precise resistance level that leaves the native grasses intact. The root mesh is easily peeled off the dome like a wrapper—leaving behind a nutrient-rich soil for the next generation of hybrid seeds. Spools are then used to capture, ravel, and transport the root mesh.

"Having mixed-grass roots inside the domes created an unparalleled phenomenon. The energy of the domes amplified and stimulated the root metropolis, while also combusting the heart valve. This evolution of energy rippled out with each tract of hybrid roots grafting, interlocking, and connecting to the native patches.

"The Mera Lab technicians also found ways to carefully harvest the blue droplets from the delicate shrubs in Settlers' Hills and use them to create a proprietary formula for fertilizer. Finally, an underground energy generator constructed beneath Settlers' Hills accelerates the growth of the hybrids.

"Son, the result of the Council's efforts was an efficient turnkey operation of root-mesh production within Settlers' Hills. Our small town makes enough root mesh that once-barren lands across the country now have newly parked sod gripping to them."

Peet's curiosity on this subject satisfied for now, he asked his father yet another complex question. "Dad, how does a motor work?"

Ansel put his glasses back on and reached for his newspaper.

Peet then stood up and stretched. "Well, I figured you were on a roll," he said, smirking. "Boy, you really are an engineer."

Ansel had shared with Peet all he knew about the efforts of the Council to protect the root metropolis. Yet, for all their talk about harvesting, fertilizing, and binding activities, neither Peet nor Ansel knew that something had changed in their environment. A hole had been punctured in their backyard, and some native roots had been torn and removed.

"Did my explanation answer your questions?" Ansel asked Peet. Before Peet could answer, Ansel continued. "I hope you now understand and appreciate why our community has the responsibility it does for these grasses."

"Dinner is almost ready," Hady said as she entered the room. Peet got up and felt more tired than when he had returned from his journey earlier. He staggered down the hallway to his room, feeling the full weight of his body. He could hear his mother clanking dishes as she set the table. Once in his room, Peet opened the antique wooden chest at the foot of his bed, picked up his baseball mitt, and placed the chisel inside it. His bed looked plush and inviting. He gravitated to it, promising himself just a few minutes of rest before dinner. He climbed into bed fully clothed. Almost immediately, his eyes closed and he fell asleep.

CHAPTER FIVE

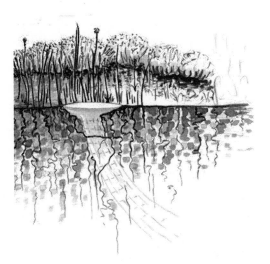

THE POND'S CHAMBER UNCOVERED

Peet awoke to Marilyn prodding his chest and bare arm with her cold, damp fingers. "Marilyn!" he said groggily. "Did you just take a bath?"

"No, not a tub bath," she giggled. "A pond bath."

Peet's eyes opened wide. "A pond bath!" he exclaimed, stricken by panic.

"Surprise!" she said excitedly. "I just filled it with water so now Jinko has a pond to bathe in!"

"What?"

"Don't you remember? You fell asleep before dinner. Mom and Dad told me not to wake you last night!"

Peet leapt up, accidentally whipping Marilyn across the bed like a rag doll. He ran into the kitchen to see if he could view the gaping hole in the ground from the patio door. Marilyn ran after him. Unable to stop on the kitchen tile with her socks, she bumped into him. "What did I do?" she asked.

"I don't see the pond from here, so that's good," Peet said. "I may have time to cover it before Mom and Dad see it."

"Weren't we going to build a pond for Jinko?" Marilyn asked.

"Yes, and 'we' means more than one person. Don't you remember? We planned to build it on the day of a full moon, then cover it the next day. Full moons usually occur twelve times a year, so we probably won't even have one this week. We have to cover it before anyone sees it. Where are Mom and Dad now?"

"Calm down, Peet," she responded. "Dad's working on the car in the garage, and Mom's out running errands."

"Help me find a calendar," Peet said, while rummaging through a kitchen drawer full of documents.

Marilyn found one and pulled it out. She followed her finger to the current day and noted it showed a full-moon symbol. "Peet! Peet! It's going to be a full moon tonight. Do you know what that means? Jinko is going to turn green today."

"Marilyn, full moon, quarter moon, or no moon, we should cover the hole and replant the pulled grasses," he said regretfully.

"We don't have to do it right now," she said with a smirk. "Come on, Peet. It's just one more day."

"Well, let's go see what damage you've really done," he

replied. Marilyn flashed him an irritated look. Before going out to the backyard, Peet phoned Jill and then Ray, asking them both to rush over. As he walked out into the yard, Marilyn closely shadowed him. Peet hoped she had not dug deep enough to cause irreparable damage to the native roots.

Peet could see a shiny reflection in the distance, behind the shrubs. It was a tinfoil, doll-sized mirror attached to a toy golf cart. He ran over to the shrubs and saw the dollhouse estate partially surrounding the clay pond. The spot for the pond was completely devoid of grass. Marilyn called his name several times, but got no reaction. Peet heard only the voices of the Genets warning him about the frailty of the root metropolis and the spirit of the Whimsical Tree.

Jill soon arrived, and found both Marilyn and Peet sitting sadly on the curb in front of their house, near the mailbox. "So, why the long faces?" she asked.

"Let's wait for Ray, then I'll explain," Peet replied. Jill sat down next to them and toyed with her phone.

Ray arrived moments later.

"What's going on?" he asked.

"It's best just to show you," Peet responded as he led the group to the pond.

"For starters, we have a gaping hole near the border of our backyard, clawed out by this 'wonder muscles' sister of mine."

"What!" Ray exclaimed.

As Jill approached the pond, her eyebrows raised, her lips tightened, and a single dimple formed on her right cheek.

"You've disrupted the native roots! I thought we planned to do this together so we didn't harm the root-metropolis system. That was the whole point." Peet and Marilyn looked down at the ground. Jill could see how distraught they were, and decided not to say anything further. A profound silence momentarily poured over them, until Peet informed them that the moon would be full that evening.

"Stop overreacting, Jill. Look, it's already done, so let's just make the most of it," Ray stated assuringly. "Tomorrow, we'll replant the grasses without anyone ever noticing they were pulled. So few were pulled that maybe they'll graft quickly." Although Peet and Jill had their reservations about his plan, they knew he was logically right, so they nodded in agreement. "Okay, good. Let's secure the pot in its place, add more water, and wait for Jinko to show." Ray gave the command with military precision.

All but Peet responded through action. "You don't understand," Peet said worriedly. "We have permanently scarred the heart of the root metropolis."

"Look, Peet. Tomorrow morning we'll remove the clay cover from the hole and patch the ground," Ray said. "Marilyn, what did you do with the roots?"

"I put them in a garbage bag and folded them in half so they would fit," Marilyn responded.

"What!" Jill exclaimed.

"Hold on. What did you do with the bag?" Ray asked.

"I put it inside the barbeque grill," Marilyn responded.

Ray, Jill, and Peet knew the roots might suffocate if the grill was full of ashes. All the kids stampeded toward the grill. Ray arrived first and threw open the grill door, only to find an ash-covered bag full of semi-limp grasses jumbled in the base of the grill. Jill dusted off the ashes and moved the bag into the shed instead.

When Jill returned, she told them, "There is nothing to do now but wait and hope the bundle of grasses will reattach when we replant them tomorrow. When did you pull them, Marilyn?" Jill asked, remembering the condition and color of the roots in the bag.

"Um, a couple of days ago," Marilyn said.

"We need to replant them as soon as possible," Jill said. "Definitely no later than tomorrow."

It was going to be a long night, so Peet suggested that Ray and Jill ask their parents for permission to spend the night. That way each of them could take a shift that evening to watch the pond for Jinko's appearance.

Later that evening, Peet and Marilyn convinced their parents to turn in early so they could privately watch a movie on the big-screen television in the family room. Jill and Ray had grown up with Peet and Marilyn, and Ansel and Hady adored them as if they were their own children. As Hady bid them goodnight, she mentioned she had prepared snacks, including a tray of homemade fudge. The children flocked to the kitchen, and soon all of their fingers were fully embedded in the fudge. Marilyn swung her dangling feet wildly under the table, clearly enjoying the fudge. Other than the noise of the movie and Jill requesting the milk carafe, the back of the house was quiet. All four of them were cautiously excited to get a glimpse of Jinko that night. Once the tray was nearly empty and their midsections full, they turned off all the lights in the back of the house. Jill, an avid camper, headed outside to set up the Sepvans' lightweight dome tent, which she found in the shed. While she assembled it in a spot between the shed and the pond, the others gathered supplies for the night.

One by one, each carrying supplies, they arrived at the tent. They set their sleeping bags parallel to one another and laid down, all eight eyes peering out at the pond. Their plan was to camp all night if necessary, though they took breaks to enjoy some of the other snacks Hady had left for them. After several hours, their excitement waned and they grew tired. Suddenly, Jinko appeared in the shadows and—with one smooth, gigantic, graceful leap—made his way next to the water. He dropped a foot inside it. At once, all the kids rolled tightly into each other, forming a single bundle. They simultaneously propped their bodies up as best they could, to better view the pond.

"No one would believe this if they didn't see it for themselves," Peet said. "Who would possibly imagine..."

"Shhh," the other kids whispered, as they had never seen Jinko before and didn't want to frighten him away. He was handsome and uniquely shaped. The image of the chalk-white frog with his emerald eyes, now swimming beneath a full moon in a multicolored clay pool filled with water, was a masterful vision of beauty.

"Good job on that pond, Marilyn," Ray said.

"Thanks," she replied. She nudged her brother.

Shortly after Jinko dove into the pond on that moonlit evening, the frog's body enlarged, while the sacs along his spine shrank considerably. This surprised the children, as they had believed the moon's rays would alter the color of the frog, not its size. All traces of the clay pot had disappeared underneath Jinko's now-enlarged body, and the sacs along his spine were barely visible. The pot had broken, crumbled, and fallen into the chamber below. Jinko looked in the direction of the children, as if he knew they had been watching him all along. He stood upright, with one leg on each side of the crevice, and bowed to them. The children were mesmerized by the gesture. Jinko then leaped high into the air, dropped into the chamber beneath the pond, and disappeared.

In fact, the frog had fallen into a most rare capillary, hidden beneath the native grasses. These underground capillaries had been formed when the last glaciers receded north, creating the prairies. Although very few capillaries existed on Earth, one lay dormant at the foot of the Sepvans' backyard, only to be accidentally sliced open by Marilyn when she was digging and removing the native roots.

That evening, all of the moon's rays were narrowly bundled and directed onto the pond, like a flashlight's beam. The moon's rays stimulated the nodes along the interior of the capillary, causing the whole underground capillary to awaken and expand. It was nearly endless in length, and could stretch and contract like an accordion. With the clay pot gone, the semi-exposed roots around the chamber also felt the sensation of the moon's rays. These native roots slowly began gravitating toward the center of the crevice, to protect the root metropolis.

Peet, Marilyn, Jill, and Ray crashed together at the tent door, all of them trying simultaneously to crawl out of the tent. Marilyn, being the smallest, got out quickest and arrived at the chamber first. Deep below, the ground appeared to have a clear coating along the edges, and the chamber had no visible end. Marilyn, without hesitation, dove after her newfound frog friend. Peet screamed after her, but Ray and Jill held him back to stop him from diving in. No sound came from the chamber. It was as if the ground had pulled Jinko and Marilyn to its core and swallowed them. Peet knew he had to follow his sister. He broke free from his friends and jumped into the chamber. After a brief debate, Jill and Ray followed. The children did more than affect the root metropolis within Barrenville; they had also awakened a capillary between two worlds.

Across town, Wanerhess Hoise noticed the direct light of the moon focused over the Sepvans' property. He knew it could only mean one thing—there was trouble brewing beneath the ground.

One additional creature was attracted to the bundled rays over the pond, and jumped in before the roots welded to cover the crevice.

CHAPTER SIX

VESUMIO VALLEY

The children did more than affect the root metropolis within Barrenville; they had also awakened a capillary between two worlds. Traveling down the silk-textured capillary—which appeared to be miles of a tubular root—was effortless and gradual, like unrolling a giant silk parachute against a cliff. The fibers of the tubular walls became thinner and more transparent as the children traveled farther from home. They could clearly begin to see the distinct layers of rock as they reached its end.

A series of nodes at the end of the capillary thwarted their progress, obstructing their path like pairs of strong thumbs. That brought the children to a gradual stop, until they could simply crawl out. One by one, each jumped out of the capillary and onto what appeared to be cobblestone ground below. Marilyn was the first to transition into the new world, followed by Peet, Jill, and Ray. Once they were all on the ground, they looked around and saw they were under a short, dirt tunnel somewhere high in the mountains.

"That was the best ride ever!" exclaimed Marilyn, as she wiped drool from her chin. "Hey, have any of you seen Jinko? He should be here already."

"Don't ever jump into a place you can't completely see," Peet warned. "That was very dangerous."

"Didn't you do the same thing? I mean, jump into a black hole?" Marilyn pointed out.

While the two siblings squabbled, Jill busily studied the spout of the capillary they'd just exited. "This species of plant is most remarkable," she said. "I've never read about anything like it before. It was like we were pills passing through a giant earthworm."

"Forget the worm," Ray exclaimed, pointing at a seven-foot-tall Mongolian draft horse, which had just then entered the tunnel. The horse's sheer size, muscular structure, and stoic posture were both impressive and beautiful. This magnificent horse was pulling four oversized, acorn-shaped pods behind him. As the horse drew closer to the children, they moved as one unit, back toward the capillary spout.

Noticing they were awestruck by him, the horse thrust his head back and forth, causing his mane to puff elegantly. "Let me introduce myself," he said to the gawking children. "My name is Mastive. I am here to collect you and lead you safely out of Vesumio."

"The horse talks," Marilyn said, giggling. "I knew animals could talk, and he is so pretty."

"Shhh," Ray said, poking her.

"My name is Peet and this is Marilyn, Ray, and Jill," Peet said, pointing at each of them as he said their names. "Where is Vesumio?"

"Vesumio is a mountainous region within the land of Norefole," Mastive said. "That's where we are now."

"I know geography well, but I'm not familiar with either of those places," Ray said. "Where is Norefole in relation to Barrenville, Illinois?"

"I'm afraid I don't know that region," Mastive responded.

"How did you know we were here?" Peet asked.

"A tremor occurred on this mountain, which could only mean that a rare capillary opened from your world."

"Different worlds?" Jill whispered.

"Come. Let's head out before darkness consumes these mountains. There is a pod for each of you. Hop in," Mastive said. Beyond Mastive's burly body, the children could see only blue skies and mountain peaks. They knew they were very far from home.

The children nodded to one another, in agreement to leave with him. Each of them drew open the half door of an acorn pod, which resembled single-occupant mini-carriages, and jumped inside. Each pod had a heavily cushioned, velvet-textured bench. The lining of the pods' interior walls was filled with whimsical, fluid murals, somehow personalized to the children's unique interests. Once the fourth door closed, Mastive pulled out from the tunnel, which was halfway up one of the many mountains in Vesumio. Led by the great horse, the procession of pods began its trek down the mountain.

They rode down along a path that hugged the mountain wall to their right. On their left was an amazing view of Vesumio Valley. In the belly of the valley sat a region of mountains with flat tops and layers of wide ridges along their sides. These ridges contained a variety of habitats for an unusual and diverse bounty of wildlife, with animals the older children knew were either highly endangered or extinct back home. There were many other creatures none of them recognized. There were animals on the ground, in the air, and living within the land. The collection of life in the valley was pure and glorious beyond imagination.

Marilyn popped herself half outside the acorn pod and asked Mastive, "Are there only animals here?"

"No, nibblet, we have others as well," Mastive replied.

"What others?" she asked, finding the word "nibblet" endearing.

"Norefole is a world with various, distinct terrains." The rest of the children also popped halfway out of their pods, so they could listen better. Each one is home to different Norefolian life. Among the Norefolians, there are the King, the Clades, the Stewards, the Grommels..."

"Cool, a King. But what are Clades?" Ray asked, interrupting.

"Clades have existed since the beginning of time. They are divided into five groups: the Imajs, Genets, Aras, Loomers, and a group we don't speak of much anymore—the Elicitors."

Peet instantly recognized the Genet name from his experience at the Whimsical Tree. "The Genets, you said? Are they here? Is Norefole where they come from?" All the others turned to him with surprise. Peet then patted his pocket to feel for the chisel. He exhaled when he realized it did not get lost in the capillary. He was excited to learn that someone, or something, knew of the Genets.

"Whoa. Slow down!" Mastive exclaimed. "Most of the Clades exert special powers, with the exception of the Elicitors. The Elicitors' only power is to extract the powers of the other four Clades.

"The Clades are much like you humans, with a few differences," Mastive said. The children hung on his every eloquent word, accompanying dramatic gestures, and distinct horse features. "Clades are born into this Kingdom and have powers and physical characteristics distinct to their Clade type. They all have visible receptors under their chins and on the undersides of their forearms. They can live about nine hundred years longer than humans, and their powers are closer to the raw powers of their ancestors. In many ways, the Clades are the early..."

"Pigeons! Pigeons!" Marilyn suddenly hollered. "Like back home." Peet rolled his eyes as they passed several pigeons on their way down the mountain.

"Not quite. They are a different kind of pigeon called passenger pigeons, and they no longer exist in your world," Mastive said. "Billions of them existed in the prairies and could cover the sky for hours as they flew by. Yet, as the prairie lands became fragmented, so did the great pigeon colonies. Your last of this species was given the name Martha and held in captivity until she died. I've learned a great deal about them since their arrival, and we share the same fate. My homeland was similar to the prairie; it was an open grassland called a steppe, which has very short grasses. Last I heard, my species had gone extinct in the wild in your world." He cleared his throat.

"As I was saying," Mastive continued. "Then there are the Stewards, the architects responsible for much of the Kingdom's landscape. You might know them as the Council. Our King sent them to your world to create an infrastructure to support your world's grassland biome before it was lost. They worked on the land with the heaviest concentration of native grasslands left in your world."

"That land is Barrenville," Peet whispered.

"Barrenville's native grasses, and their intoxicating nature, also attract Ascentias," Mastive continued.

"What's an Ascentia?" Peet asked, wondering what other Norefolian visitors he might have come across back home.

"Ascentias are rare and mystical creatures from Norefole who can amplify the raw powers of the Clades. We also call earthly animal species Ascentias, but only when they come close to extinction. You see, as the numbers in a species begin to dwindle, their energy intensifies exponentially in the remaining few animals. We call this type of energy Juso. The nearly extinct animals live more powerfully, with the hope of prolonging the species and minimizing the impact it will have on other species if they cease to exist. Vesumio Valley is home to many such Ascentias to help preserve the diversity of species. The shelf-like-ridges you see on the mountainsides expand and multiply to create habitat for more Ascentias as they arrive, as more space is required to maintain life."

Seeing how the children's eyes appeared glazed from overstimulation, Mastive asked, "What brings you to Norefole, my friends?"

"We followed Jinko," Marilyn said. "He is a handsome, white frog with emerald eyes."

"That sounds like a Grommel," Mastive said. "Strange, but I did not sense its presence within Vesumio Valley."

"What is a Grommel?" Marilyn asked.

"Grommels are a special breed of frogs that hunt for Ascentias and bring them here," Mastive replied. "They have six sacs along their spines, three on each side. Are you sure you followed a Grommel?"

"Yes!" they all responded.

"It must be a Grommel," Mastive whispered, intrigued. "The Grommel must have been searching for an Ascentia on your land. Yet, Grommels do not use prehistoric capillaries to travel. Even stranger is how the four of you survived the capillary. I have never met anyone who successfully used one to cross into this world."

The children looked confused. "You're probably not familiar with a capillary, are you?" Mastive asked, continuing as the children all shook their heads. "It's what you just used to enter Norefole. Capillaries can exist in their natural environment for millions of years undisturbed, but their undoing occurs in just a few days. If one is torn or opened, its textured walls will thin until they dissolve into water and spurt out of the ground. The capillary's cavity ultimately acts as a channel for the collected water, but first it will swell briefly to allow foreign matter—such as yourselves—to pass through, but rarely all the way through. It is nearly impossible to survive a journey through one, so you were very lucky; you could have suffocated.

"These capillaries are an alternative entryway into our world. Every century or so, we hear about the discovery of a rare capillary. All Norefolian Kings throughout history have ordered them mined and destroyed so that the balance of life is maintained."

"Well, we came through alright," Marilyn said.

"It sounds like we shouldn't try that again, kiddo," Jill said. When they made their final turn down the mountain and onto the last section of the path, night prevailed over the landscape and echoing calls of unfamiliar wildlife accompanied them. In the distance, a pool of lights appeared as one static light show, revealing the Kingdom.

Once they stopped, the children got out of the pods and

looked for a place to spend the night. Mastive explained that they would have to continue alone the next morning, as he could not travel beyond the valley. As they settled into sleep on large tarps found inside the benches in their pods, Mastive summarized Norefole's landscape. "The Kingdom is strategically located between several terrains. It abuts steep mountainous ranges in all directions but the east, where it borders the desert and a single region of woods. Vesumio is surrounded by Plain Desert and Cradle Desert to its west. Grommel Lake lies south of all the deserts and the Kingdom. Our expansive continent is thousands of miles long and wide, and is surrounded by ocean. Farther from here are many other smaller communities with different populations." With Mastive watching over them and exhausted from their travels, the children slept soundly through the evening.

CHAPTER SEVEN

THE JOURNEY BEGINS

The next morning, Peet, Marilyn, and Ray were awakened by Jill slapping her shoes together, trying to remove the particles of sand from inside them. She told them she had gone out to explore what Mastive called the desert cradles, which were located nearby. "We're not going to get back home anytime soon if we keep sleeping," Jill said. Given the splendor and bounty of the new world, the children had little time to reflect on home. Just then, Mastive appeared and told them it would be a day's journey to reach Grommel Lake. He instructed them to keep close to the path of desert cradles, as it would lead them to Grommel Lake, the last safe stop before they reached the Kingdom. Once they reached the Kingdom, the King could help them return home.

The base of the mountain they came from appeared to be powdered with white sand. Looking ahead, they could see three tiers of differently colored sand. The white sand gave way to custard-colored sand and then to caramel-colored sand, which dominated the scenery all the way to the horizon. Directly in front of them, the landscape appeared broken by an endless series of desert cradles that were made of black, nonporous lava rock on the outer layer, with a textured layer of mosses on the inside. The center of each cradle contained a single, four-foot-long, vertical vine that held multi-colored pods. The lava rocks absorbed heat from the desert sun, and the mosses harnessed, redirected, and cycled energy between the vine and the rocks. When the children stood close enough to the rocks, they could hear them crackling.

The shells of the pods, as well as the droplets inside, had a pomegranate-like texture. The size and shape of the pods resembled that of a papaya, and the flesh around its core was like an apple's, except lighter in weight. After a lengthy time in the desert, Ray decided to jump over the lava rocks, and landed on the moss filler. He gazed at the vibrant colors of the pods, which clung to the vine like dew drops on a petal. Ray reached into his pocket and pulled out the mini pocketknife that hung on his keychain, then pulled off a pod from the vine. With his knife, he cut deep into the pod to open it—and found several sweet, tart, salty-smelling, creamy droplets attached to the flesh. He plucked out a droplet and placed it in his mouth. Upon touching his tongue, it became everything he knew about taste, smell, and texture, and even made the crunch sound of potato pancakes, Ray's favorite dish. Marilyn, Jill, and Peet watched intently as his facial expression changed from just curious to sheer pleasure. The others dashed to find pods for themselves. Ray passed the knife to Jill, who instantly enjoyed a mouthwatering, fresh, cinnamon-laced peach cobbler. Peet opened one up for both Marilyn and himself. Both had cravings for their mother's homemade lasagna, and chewing on the thick droplets brought that memory back.

Although food and water now appeared abundant, the children had a new concern. No other life could be seen. The only sounds that emanated from the desert were the occasional whispering winds from the northwest and the constant simmering of the rocks.

As the children traveled from cradle to cradle, desert-dwelling creatures called the Mocoons noticed their presence. Mocoons were compact creatures made from threaded sand, and looked like stacks of wafers arranged in the shape of a ball. They could use the bountiful sands around them to weave paper-thin wafers and spherical shapes of any size, and each object they wove was as unique and detailed as a snowflake. The Mocoons wove themselves into these shapes of beautiful splendor to lure their prey away from the path of the cradles.

From the side of Plain Desert, a tsunami of rotating wafers of varying sizes and intricate beauty appeared before the travelers. As each new wafer came into being, there was an overpowering, deafening noise of strong winds clumping the sands together. The children's vision was greatly impaired, as in a sandstorm. Ray cautiously approached the wall of swirling visuals, with Peet and Jill following slowly behind. Peet turned back to see Marilyn standing safely near a cradle. He yelled at her to stay, but his words were in vain, and his gestures were unclear because of the chaotic whirlwind of sand debris moving through.

Marilyn noticed a peculiar set of wafers that had drifted in their direction. Soon she found herself enclosed in an elaborate, moving tunnel of thickly layered sand wafers pulling her deeper into the adjacent Plain Desert. Once Marilyn was well into Plain Desert, the other Mocoons left the area of the cradles. Slowly, the wafers of sand dissolved and cascaded back into the desert floor. Marilyn had vanished.

Peet, Ray, and Jill cried out Marilyn's name as they looked for her in every direction. They backtracked to the cradle with the blue-colored pods she had admired. When they did not find her there, they next traveled forward to the cradle where the Mocoons interrupted their journey, and then went beyond that point for a while. Marilyn was nowhere to be found. The three of them considered traveling back to Vesumio Valley to find Mastive, but realized they were too far away and that Mastive could not travel beyond Vesumio.

They split up and spent the next several hours searching the deserts. Eventually, they regrouped back at the cradle where they had last seen Marilyn. Peet arrived last with a look of despair on his face, fearing she would never be found. He slumped down to his knees when he noticed Jill and Ray stood alone near the cradle. Ray ran over to console his friend. He pressed his hand firmly on Peet's shoulder, assuring him they would not rest until they found her. The two of them gazed back at Jill, who was clearly upset and frustrated, looking back at them and the endless desert around them.

"She's all alone out there," Peet said. "How could she have disappeared on us again?"

"I know, Peet, but we need to keep moving," Ray said. "We need guides, supplies...We don't know these deserts. We need help now more than ever." Peet knew Ray was right, but he wanted to stay behind and wait for her there. They spent the next half hour debating whether Peet should stay behind. Ultimately, they voted, and soon the three of them continued south on the path of the cradles.

They quietly walked in solace for many miles. Finally, on the distant horizon, the sunburned children saw an enormous limestone bluff. As they neared, the desert sands thinned until they were on full dirt ground. They headed into the bluff's slit opening. Inside, it looked like a fortress. In the center was a shallow, oblong pond that occupied nearly all of the ground inside. The structure was several stories high, and its interior had hundreds of small caverns.

Peet, Jill, and Ray stood in amazement at what occupied the caverns—hundreds of emerald-eyed, white frogs with the height, weight, and strength of a large dog, like a Labrador. Although the frogs varied slightly in size and shape, they all had sacs along their spines, exactly like Jinko's. Peet knew they couldn't turn away without being noticed, so he yelled out for Jinko. His high voice echoed throughout the interior of the bluff. The hundreds of frogs immediately went silent, and all their jewel-like eyes turned to observe Peet, Jill, and Ray. A few larger frogs with artillery bands around their waists approached them. One of them, named Grog, leapt directly in front of them, startling the children. "Who is Jinko, and why do you yell?" he asked.

"Ummm... Jinko looks like you," Peet responded nervously, "but with a brown spot on his shoulder."

Grog smiled and nodded. "Ah, yes. Your Jinko is our Gromyko."

"I named him Jinko when I discovered him in our backyard," Peet said. "I am Peet, and this is Ray and Jill. We are from Barrenville."

"Ah yes, Barrenville, the heart of the grasslands," Grog said. He appeared to bask in the sound of the Barrenville name. "How did you get here?"

The children explained how what had started as a well-intentioned project to build a pond for Gromyko had led them to discover the rare capillary beneath it.

"You tore out the native roots in Barrenville to carve out a pond?" Grog stated, shaking his head in disbelief. The children nodded.

"Yes, then we followed Gromyko down the capillary, which led us to your world," Ray said.

"It's impossible for a Grommel not to find his way back to Grommel Lake," Grog replied. "Why would Gromyko have used a death trap of a capillary, rather than a customary aerial bridge between our worlds?"

Grog pulled away and bowed his head with grave concern, wondering why Gromyko had not yet returned home from Barrenville. After all, these humans had come from there at the same time Gromyko had left. Grog drew closer to the humans to better assess them. The children went on to describe their journey through the desert to Grommel Lake, and how they'd lost Marilyn during a magical sandstorm.

"It looks like we'll be working together to rescue Marilyn and find Gromyko," Grog said. "It's best you get comfortable here." More Grommels, not part of the troop wearing belts, slowly approached the children. Many of the Grommels had never laid eyes on humans before, and found them a curious species.

Before Peet could ask about their plan to find Marilyn and Gromyko, he heard a female voice call him. "How did Gromyko appear to you?" inquired a concerned Grommel named Grayle.

"We thought he was ill because we'd never seen a white frog before," Peet said. "His skin looked pale and weathered, which is why we created a pond in the first place. He swam in our pond during a full moon and then he got much bigger. Your size, in fact."

Grayle smiled. "We can alter our size through the use of our sacs, without exposure to the moon. Gromyko merely adjusted to his environment to fit the need at the moment." Peet now better understood how Gromyko had nearly disappeared into the crevice under the gutter guard in his backyard.

"He didn't start as big as all of you," Jill said. "He was tiny in comparison."

"You are in Norefole now, and this is our normal size," Grayle said. "Outside of Norefole, we can shrink ourselves to the size of one of your world's frogs. Fellow Grommels, please, let's not crowd the humans." Grayle waved her hands to the growing crowd.

The Grommels moved back and apart, giving the children a full view of a magnificent vase rotating at the far end of the pond. As it rotated, each side of the vase portrayed distinct images of Earth, never repeating. The children gasped for breath as they beheld the simple beauty of the unique but complex vase. The children also noticed the relatively short distance between the interior of the bluff and the pond.

"Is this Grommel Lake?" Ray asked, referring to the fortress.

"Yes," Grog said. "It was constructed by our first ancestors, carved out of limestone. It is our protection from the vast deserts and Barren Woods."

Grog then looked sternly at the children and said, "You are absolutely prohibited from touching the vase or getting anywhere near the waters of this pond. It is off limits!"

"You need not be that strict, father," Grayle said to Grog. She then turned to the children. "The vase emulates and reflects all the life zones of Earth. We safeguard it here from the Cone Witch, the Elicitors, and others who might want to use it to gain access to our aerial bridges. Access to those bridges is access to a source of power that could help them conquer our world. Do you understand?"

"There is a witch!" Ray exclaimed. All three children looked at one another.

"Good, then," Grog murmured. He motioned for one of his battalion heads to approach.

Grople stepped forward. "Grommel Lake is the vase's sanctuary," he explained. "The vase reflects the health of both our worlds, and represents the Earth's rawest qualities in real time. It rotates eternally, always spinning a continuous thread from an interior core of Earth's sediment, using prehistoric biomass from the thick network of grass roots. This vase evolved into the heart valve of Norefole, just as Barrenville's root metropolis evolved into the heart valve of Earth's grassland biome. Thus, the health of your biomes has a direct impact on our eternally rotating vase.

"In the universal matrix, Earth is merely another continent to Norefole, separated by galactic matter instead of oceans. Hence, our worlds are connected, and any substantial affliction in one world has a corresponding effect on the other. As the grassland biome has been compromised over time, the color of the vase gradually lost its luster, and it became spotted. Occasionally, as it spins, sections of the vase walls appear scarred, thinner, and with indentations. Like the vase, we Grommels also reflect the overall health of all life in our mutual worlds. The thick webbing we once had around our fingers has weakened and become spotted. Our six sacs have also lost some of their elasticity.

"The grassland biome, greatly rebuilt through hybrids, stabilized the integrity of the vase—until recently. The day before you children came to Grommel Lake, we noticed something unusual, a red thread circulating within the vase. It could only mean the fabric of the dual-heart valve in Barrenville had been torn. The strength of the root metropolis is what has naturally kept your land mass bonded, anchored your continent to Earth's waters, and helped keep our vase alive.

"The vase also materializes aerial bridges that connect our worlds," Grayle said. "This allows us to transport Ascentias from your world to this one for preservation, and to send Stewards to secure your biomes. Our ancestors learned how to travel between our worlds, and passed that secret knowledge from one Grommel generation to the next." The children were amazed to learn about the exchanges between worlds right under their very noses.

"Will the bridges always lead back here?" Jill asked.

"All bridges into Norefole end here in Grommel Lake," Grayle responded.

"If more threads in the vase turn red, the vase will destabilize, and life on Earth as well as life in Norefole will never be the same again," Grople continued. "Our pond's waters will turn to silt, preventing the vase from spinning and causing the vase to harden. Then the aerial bridges will collapse, making Norefole inaccessible to your world. Any Ascentias stranded in your world would then be lost to the universe forever."

"We nearly lost the most powerful Ascentia of your grassland biome, the Regal Deer," Grog said. "A fellow Norefolian, Wanerhess Hoise, notified us that the last Regal Deer was seen feeding in Barrenville's rich prairie. Any species near extinction instinctually gravitates to its biome's richest resource. For grasslands, that meant Barrenville's intoxicating grasses. We intended to retire the Regal Deer in Vesumio.

"Somehow other Norefolians came to know about the Regal Deer, and soon it became a race to find it. Unfortunately, one of the Cone Witch's brood, a Mocoon, found a way to infiltrate Grommel Lake. It lived among us secretly, learning how to use the vase and access the aerial bridge. One day, the Mocoon smuggled the Cone Witch into our fortress and opened an aerial bridge that led them directly to Barrenville. The next day, we found remnants of fragmented cone chips and grains of sand floating in the aerial bridge and immediately notified the King of the security breach. He sent one of our most skilled Loomers, as well as three Genets and Gromyko, to locate the Cone Witch and prevent her from reaching the last Regal Deer."

"Why would the Witch want a deer?" Ray asked.

"Because it is a key species of the grassland biome, an Ascentia with a most unique and potent Juso," Grog said. "Feeding on its Juso would give her the strength and power she needs to overthrow the King and conquer Norefole. If the Elicitors, who have sided with the Witch, acquired the deer's power, they would be able to keep forever all the powers they elicited from another Clade. That would make them a lethal force against their own fellow Clades.

"The Cone Witch and our Loomer, disguised as a hunter, tried to capture the deer at the same time. The Loomer was about to dart the deer for sleep, so he could transport it here, but the Witch intervened. The deer's resistance to the Witch's powers caused her to break her collarbone. That made her vulnerable to capture by the Loomer, so she retreated using the same aerial bridge she came in on. She returned partially defeated, but she had managed to turn the Regal Deer into a tree, preventing the Clades or Gromyko from moving it to Vesumio, where she would never be able to reach it. The Loomer had stopped the Witch from stealing the deer's powers that day, but she vowed to someday return and claim them. Because the Witch knew the Regal Deer's location, the three Genets stayed to guard it.

"It's getting late, and I need time to organize the search," Grog said, feeling anxious and restless about Gromyko. "Grayle, please show them to their caverns."

Peet immediately declined. "I can't rest until I find my sister. She's out there in the desert with those creatures. If only I had watched her more carefully." His eyes welled up with tears.

"We will find her," Grayle said softly into Peet's ear, "just as we will find Gromyko."

Grog nodded to five of the larger Grommels, the battalion heads, who promptly called for unit formation. Beyond the cavern entrance, the Grommel troops, all with their distinctive belts, arranged themselves in five groups of twenty. They were nearly all identical to Gromyko, Peet thought as they passed by him.

A parallel troop of caramel-colored lizards met the Grommels outside. With the Grommels mounted, Grog bellowed, "Comb the deserts for Gromyko, who has returned to Norefole, and for Marilyn the human, who earlier today was taken from Cradle

59

Desert." They traveled into the desert in a diamond formation, with Grog leading the way.

Grayle rounded up the three tired children and nudged them to follow her. The children followed quietly. She led them to three of the hundreds of ornately framed crevices within the interior of the bluff. Peet, Jill, and Ray each had their own cavern on the ground level, where they found an oversized, circular, cushioned pad and a small pool with a delicate waterfall spring. Each child took hold of several differently textured pillows on the pad, and basked in the scent of calming incense and the sound of the waterfall. Almost as quickly as the children rested on their pillows, they each fell asleep.

CHAPTER EIGHT

UNREST IN NOREFOLE

The Mocoon had led Marilyn through an illusion of tunnels, paths, and rooms, until they arrived at their village deep into Plain Desert. What had started as a slow skip turned into a run, as each passage became more beautiful and whimsical. Once at the village, the Mocoon placed Marilyn in a sand hut, then alerted its master that they had arrived. Marilyn was thirsty from running in the desert, and asked for water. The Mocoon, however, could not provide any water, as there was none in Plain Desert. Instead, it tried to distract her by creating opulent displays of fireworks from the sand. Marilyn eventually realized no water would come, and began to cry. More Mocoons gathered around and, together, they created a theatrical performance of dancing, playful sculptures that filled nearly every corner of her hut. Through all the sand dust, clumps, and objects, Marilyn instead found comfort in the moonbeams hitting her arm from the window above. The Mocoons left her alone in the hut, but not before creating a sand bed.

Marilyn settled into the bed and gazed out the window at the moon, which appeared much larger and closer than the one back home. As she coiled her body, she placed her hands in her pockets and discovered three droplets left over from a blue pod she had opened in Cradle Desert. She had forgotten she placed them in her pocket well before she saw the architectural spectacles constructed by the Mocoons. She smiled, holding the droplets with care and purpose. She envisioned a traditional Thanksgiving turkey with all the savory trimmings, and a massive pitcher of ice water with lemon slices. She placed the first droplet into her mouth, and memories of all the flavors, textures, and smells of that Thanksgiving meal came rushing back to her. Moments later, she was even hit with post-Thanksgiving bellyache and sleepiness. She decided to keep the other two droplets for another day.

As she slept, three Elicitors entered the room. The Elicitors were tall, lean, and cloaked in dark burgundy. Their faces were long, their round eyes large, and their eyebrows eerily slanted. The Elicitors schemed about how to use their captive. After all, she came from another world, and her kind did not exist in Norefole. Although they didn't know what powers she had, if any, they still argued about who was going to take them.

Marilyn was awakened by their high-pitched voices, which sounded to her like steel blades clashing against one another. It sounded as if their words were spoken in the future and disassembled like a tossed salad before they became cohesive sentences. She cleaned out some sand from her ears to listen better. Finally, she sat up in the corner of the bed with her arms tightened around her legs.

"Who are you?" she asked in a very shy voice. She was slightly frightened, but more curious about these unusual-looking beings.

"Ah, the child has awoken," the first Elicitor said. "It is not who we are that matters, but rather what power you possess."

"What power?" Marilyn asked, thinking that perhaps they wanted to take her last magical droplets. "I don't have any powers."

"I'm quite certain she is tired from her travels, and we should try to make her more comfortable," another Elicitor said.

"Will you help me find my brother and friends tomorrow?" Marilyn asked, observing the three of them carefully.

The Mocoon had already informed the Elicitors that three humans remained on the path, heading in the direction of Grommel Lake. They all smirked. "Of course we will," one said. "But you must rest up for tomorrow's search. Will it help if we sing you back to sleep?" Marilyn nodded.

"Now, fellow Elicitors, let's give her a good night's rest," another Elicitor said. "Perhaps if she feels at home, she will be more willing to share what she knows—and that which she does not know. In that way, we can get to know her better." The two other Elicitors nodded, and all three began to sing in the unified voice of a glorious choir. The Mocoons followed suit, harmonizing with the Elicitors' song. With their singing they reconfigured the space they were in, from a small hut to an elaborate opera house with heavenly acoustics. Marilyn's bed was transformed into a back pew of the opera house. The soothing and restful music enveloped her, and slowly she drifted back to sleep.

* * *

The next morning at Grommel Lake, Peet awoke early and refreshed himself in the crevice's waterfall. Grayle had prepared baskets of assorted Norefolian fruits and nuts for the visitors, and left one right outside each of their caverns. The horns above some of the crevices filled the air with a sound that carried through the fortress, waking everyone. Grog and one unit had returned. Ray and Jill woke with the horn blast and stepped out onto the track surrounding the lake. The Grommels leaped from every direction to the ground. First Peet, then Ray and Jill, made their way toward the entrance to join the growing crowd of Grommels. While the Grommels were scrambling among the troops, the children pushed their way into the crowd, hoping to also reach Grog and hear the news. The horn sounded a second time.

"Everyone quiet, please," Grog announced. "We were unable

to find Marilyn or Gromyko last night." Only whispers filled his pause. "However, the sand composition near one particular cradle trails into Plain Desert, which confirms Marilyn was taken by the Mocoons. And, while trekking near the outskirts of Plain Desert alongside Vesumio Valley, we found Gromyko's belt."

There was one unanimous gasp from the Grommels as Grog held up the belt. "No! No!" Grog said as he hopped off his lizard. "Let's not jump to conclusions. We all know Gromyko is one of our best warriors, and in that we must trust." The crowd of Grommels dispersed slowly, many whispering in hushed tones as they returned to their caverns. Grayle approached Grog and handed him a robe. The rest of the Grommel troop jumped in the lake to cool off and prepare for a second, longer trip through Plain Desert.

The children approached Grog, who was receiving reports from Grople, who had returned earlier. Upon seeing the children, Grog nodded to them and stressed that although they had not yet found Marilyn, other troops were still out searching. He also assured them that the Mocoons would not hurt Marilyn. They would believe she was an Ascentia with Juso or have a power, and report it back to the Witch.

"Let's hope we can get to Gromyko and Marilyn before the Witch finds them," Grog said.

"Powers? What powers?" Ray asked. "If we had powers, we would all be back in Barrenville."

"And what if they also captured Jinko? I mean, Gromyko?" Peet asked.

"If they know Gromyko had returned from your land, they would want to extract knowledge from him," Grog said, with heartfelt sentiment. "Otherwise, they have no use for him, and they would trap him in the desert until he dried to death. A Grommel cannot survive long in the desert. We've lost many Grommels this way."

With a great whirring sound like a flock of hummingbirds, two Grommels came through the aerial bridge, in the direction of Grog, Peet, Jill, and Ray. The children were astounded to see a bridge protruding from the vase. As the bridge materialized, they also watched the transition and transformation of the returning Grommels. While in the vase, the Grommels had plump side sacs on thin bodies. Yet, as they transitioned away from the bridge and onto land, their sacs became exponentially smaller, and their bodies became larger.

"Sir Grog!" the scruffier of the two Grommels said, "The Regal Deer is still in position and Wanerhess was right about the black-tailed prairie dog." As the Grommel unclipped his harness from his belt and set it on the ground, the two cinnamon-colored, squirrel-like critters at the other end of the harness began to wriggle. The prairie dogs were suspended by long, wavy, free-floating, magnetic straps. Next, a porter Grommel called for his desert lizard. He strapped on the harness holding the Ascentias, and rode off to take them to Vesumio Valley.

"Does this really lead to Barrenville?" Jill asked, pointing at the vase.

Grog nodded. "The King is the gatekeeper of the vase and the aerial bridges, and we are their guardians. We cannot allow anyone through unless it is granted by the King," Grog said. "We will find Marilyn, but you must continue to the Kingdom if you wish to get home again."

"Then we will be on our way," Ray said.

"Wait. The Mocoons will now be waiting for you in the shadows of Plain Desert, so you must use our lizards to avoid them," Grog said. "The lizards will take you to the edges of the desert, at the foot of Barren Woods—the home of the Cone Witch. Reptiles cannot traverse the unnatural terrain of Barren Woods, so you will have to walk from there to the Kingdom."

Although their stay at Grommel Lake had been short, the children felt great affection for the Grommels, especially for Grayle, who had been protective and nurturing since their arrival. Other Grommels also approached them to say their goodbyes. Soon the children were back at the entrance to the bluff. As they mounted the lizards, Grog gave them one last, stern warning. "Stay together and keep away from the Cone Witch and her young," he said. Grog slapped the harness of Peet's lizard with his tongue, and the lizards darted out at a near sprint. It was not yet noon, and a two-thirds moon hung clearly visible in the daytime sky.

*   *   *

As the Elicitors nearly completed their last of several songs—while watching Marilyn's every gesture, blink, and shift in position—the Cone Witch appeared. She had a long, sculpted face with large, round, gray eyes, a short, pointed nose, and small lips. Her arms and legs were long and thin. The full length of her long thighs up to part of her waist was covered with pinecone scales that billowed out like a skirt. Her skin was pale, except for the rustic cone color around her waist and thighs. She was eerily beautiful, yet deadly and wicked.

Rather than feeling rested, Marilyn awoke from her deep sleep with a sense of exhaustion. She opened her eyes and gasped: the Witch was standing right in front of her. The mere proximity of the Witch depleted Marilyn's strength, and she felt weak. The Witch waved her thin arm, and the Elicitors ceased their haunting, mesmerizing song. "She is very supple and young. My woods will enjoy her," she said in a stern, strong monotone. As she bent down to Marilyn's side to view her better, the Witch let out a painful scream, and several scales along her back splintered. Marilyn also screamed, but from fright. The Witch could sense that foreign life was in her woods; something or someone had harmed one of her seedlings, causing her scales to break.

Only a few of her seedlings nested in Barren Woods, mixed in among the countless regular seedlings. Yet, one of her own had been found and partially crushed. "The child has had enough entertainment for one day!" she said contemptuously to the Elicitors. "Take her to the chambers. I'll deal with this one later." Then, as quickly as she appeared, she was gone. The opera house trickled away.

The Mocoons took Marilyn to the opposite side of the village and into a sand chamber. Once Marilyn was inside, the opening sealed so that it appeared to be a solid wall again. Soon, something or someone began to scramble under a pile of burlap blankets in the corner. Marilyn thought it was a Mocoon, so she called for it. No answer. It stood still. Then, the creature in the corner slowly stood up. She became infinitely frightened, as the stranger was much taller than a Mocoon, though not as tall as an Elicitor or the Cone Witch. Marilyn's eyes grew wider as she watched its form stretch. As the stranger pulled off the blankets, she saw a teenage-looking fellow. The stranger saw Marilyn pressed against the opposite wall, with one eye visible between her fingers. "Don't be frightened," he said. Marilyn could see the sincerity of his eyes and his kind, young face.

"Who are you?" she asked, more calmly.

"My name is Al'Bual, and I am a Loomer."

"A Loomer Clade!" she exclaimed, recalling Mastive telling her that all the Clades but the Elicitors sided with the King.

"Did they capture you too?"

"Yes."

"How?"

"In one of my youthful travels, I came across Plain Desert, where I found the Mocoon village. As a Clade, I was warned never to travel in Plain Desert, but my curiosity for relics got the best of me. I put the entire Kingdom at risk through my immature, archaeological ambitions. An Elicitor, who had stolen Genet powers at the time, sensed my energy near the village and notified the Witch. When I returned to re-enter my body, she was waiting outside the Kingdom, near the place where I'd left my body resting. The Witch has kept me prisoner here ever since, waiting for me to mature so she can use my powers."

"Wait, you were separate from your body?" she inquired.

"Yes. We Loomers have always had the ability to separate from our physical bodies, loom in their shadows, and even travel beyond those shadows. While our bodies remain stationary and our minds quiet, our energy mass disengages from our bodies, like shedding our clothes, allowing us to loom and move with purpose. Our travel capabilities have no range or limits."

"Do all the Clades look like you?" Marilyn asked, noticing the oddity of spots under his chin and on the undersides of his forearms.

"No, each of the five Clades has different characteristics, as well as different powers. The Imajs have larger, wider-set eyes, which suits their visual powers. Their faces are unusually wide and flat, and they are about as tall as we Loomers. Imajs can materialize life forms and objects from visions they see. They find shapes and figures on solid and busy textures—like textiles, stone, glass, or wood—and extract them.

"Then there are the Genets, nearly half the height of the Imajs. Genets are slender and compact in build, and they are skillful seekers and miners of energy. There are the Aras, who are the tallest of the Clades because of their long thighs. They are lanky in form and slinky in movement, and they can distinguish and measure the quality of any life form through the natural aura it produces. All living creatures produce auras of different colors

70

and strengths, and Aras can transform auras into tangible, physical bands that act like shields.

"The Elicitors are the most versatile of the Clades because they can take the powers of the others—but only for a single use. Once the power they've taken has served its purpose, it extinguishes. Because their only real power is taking the power of others, the Elicitors were always susceptible to exploitation by someone like the Witch.

"They were once the Clade closest to the King. The Elicitors lived peacefully within the Kingdom with the other four Clades. Together, we formed a perfectly harmonious sphere of energy—a universal, euphoric perfection of mixed energies, reached through the Clades' use of powers. If part of the sphere defected, the whole sphere suffered, as happened when the Witch enticed the Elicitors to abandon the Kingdom and align with her. She promised them something the King would never do—she promised to alter the Elicitors' powers permanently. The King refused to alter any of the Clade powers because it would shift the balance of energies."

"Has the Witch changed their powers?" Marilyn asked.

"No, but she uses that promise to keep their allegiance, which the Witch requires in order to someday conquer the Kingdom. We hope that before the day comes, the Elicitors will voluntarily return to the Kingdom in peace."

A Mocoon guard heard Marilyn and the Loomer talking. The Mocoon transformed itself into a sawmill blade and rolled inside the chamber to silence them. Once it got their attention, it rolled

71

out again.

"If we could break free, then we could travel to the Kingdom," Al'Bual whispered. "Do you have any powers, human?"

"Ummm...Um... I have droplets, and I can color anything," she said.

"Anything?" he asked.

"I can even dye sand," Marilyn replied.

CHAPTER NINE

THE CONE WITCH

At the same time Marilyn encountered the Cone Witch, Peet, Jill, and Ray had crossed into Barren Woods. The woods were speckled by a few pines and full of countless barren trees, which had dramatically pointing branches. Some of the leafless trees looked youthful because of how tall, smooth, and lean they were; others showed their age through their thick masses, knobs, and prickliness. Twigs, fallen branches, and several varieties of pine cones made up the forest floor, which spread across countless plateaus.

Jill, a keen forest manager in the making, picked up a most unusual cone partially embedded in the ground. She noticed it was solid and heavy, with a felt-like texture. Jill looked up at the trees around her, and noticed the cone did not match the only nearby pine. Peet and Ray had gone ahead of her, so she placed the cone into her pocket, first ripping off one of its scales to feel its coarseness.

The only noise to be heard was the children trekking through the forest. Soon a light fog came between them. A haunting feeling enveloped the woods, and a sense of despair and emptiness crept into their hearts. Ray saw what appeared to be an oddly shaped shadow of a heavily fleshed pine tree. Curiously, he approached the shadow, moving in a different direction than Jill and Peet. As he separated from the others and came closer to the pine tree, he felt an intense pull toward it. He stood alone in its shadow, and from there he could see an oddly elongated cone on a plateau nearby. The cone began to swivel. The temperature dropped significantly, and the air became frosty. All Ray could do was tremble, from fright and cold.

The Cone Witch had been sitting on the edge of one of the many plateaus. Her thin legs and arms spun in Ray's direction as she turned to face him. Her eyes were strikingly beautiful and her energy was undeniably alluring, but Ray sensed that something was very wrong. He tried to call out for Peet and Jill, but could not. He was bewildered by the contrast of the Witch's smooth skin against the coarse, formidable scales that fully lined her billowing cone shape. As he gazed into her bright eyes and delicate facial features, he felt his limbs getting heavier and more rigid, until they became lifeless and impossible to move. The

Witch was preparing Ray for encapsulation into a barren tree. The more he tried to break free, the quicker his limbs transformed into wood, starting with his toes and fingers.

Jill turned to look for Ray, thinking he had been suspiciously quiet, and realized he was gone. She alerted Peet, and they backtracked while calling Ray's name. Their cries reverberated throughout the forest, but no response came. Ray was nowhere to be found.

The fog thickened, until Jill and Peet could only hear the tail ends of their exchanges. The Cone Witch knew that she could more easily subdue her prey if she caught each one alone and by surprise. Walking blindly through the fog, Peet felt the eerie and significant drop in temperature. A cold blast made him shiver and caused the thicket of the fog to subside. Then, what appeared to be a gigantic pinecone spun in his direction and abruptly stopped right in front of him. Peet was stunned as he observed the unveiling and unraveling of this creature. He felt his ankles, kneecaps, elbows, and knuckles starting to lengthen, before the feeling gave way to numbness.

When Jill realized Peet was gone too, she instinctively knew to continue moving in the opposite direction from which they came. Although she had a good sense of direction, the fog prevented her from seeing any clearing from the woods. Suddenly, a cold gust parted the fog, revealing the Cone Witch marching toward her. Jill's limbs quickly turned dense and became challenging to control. At the same time, Jill realized the cone in her pocket had scales of the same type and color as the Cone Witch's. Before her arm became completely disabled, Jill grasped the cone in her pocket and, clenching it tightly, held it out before the Witch. Seeing the cone in Jill's hand, the Witch's eyes widened in sheer horror. Jill felt the Witch's grip on her release.

"I demand you return that to me," the Witch snarled.

"Not until you let us leave here safely!" Jill yelled back with the same ferocity, now realizing the cone was the key for her and her friends to escape. While Jill had the cone in her hand, the Witch could not harm her without risking damage to her seedling.

"It's too late for your friends," the Witch said with a sarcastic smile. "They are germinating, and the cool infusion of the fog's moisture will integrate them into my forest. In a few days, they shall live as barren trees for all eternity. You will never see them again." Jill felt the words running through her body like electrical currents. She looked more closely at the trees and realized, for the first time, that most of them were different lives transformed into trees by the Witch. Jill herself was only moments away from becoming one of them. The fog had greatly dissipated, but the air was still cool. Jill could now see the Kingdom in the distance, and the Cone Witch noticed.

"You may now hand me my seedling and be off on your way to the Kingdom. You may not have saved your friends, but you can still save yourself."

Jill carefully watched the Witch while she spoke, and noticed she had a wide gap in the middle of her collarbone. "I'm keeping it until you return my friends to me," Jill said, believing they could still be restored to themselves.

Aggravated with Jill, the Witch stomped toward her. Scared, Jill tightened her grip on the cone she was holding and accidentally broke off another scale. The Witch shrieked from pain and momentarily coiled her arms and legs. She retreated back into the woods, warning Jill that her friends would certainly die if any more harm came to the cone. Her last words to Jill echoed in the woods, "I promise we will meet again, and sooner than you think." Once the Witch had gone, the fog became a light mist near the perimeter of Barren Woods, and the air warmed up again.

Jill knew she had to move ahead, even without Peet and Ray, so she walked briskly in the direction of the Kingdom. When she felt she was out of danger, she slumped over a boulder and began to cry. She had been brave in the woods, but now felt defeated. How was she going to save her friends from the Witch, let alone find Marilyn?

The fear of being completely alone in a strange land lifted when two strikingly unusual individuals approached her—an Imaj and an Ara, both robed in beautiful, shimmering garments.

"This human has suffered a heavy loss," the Ara said. Jill was startled by the Ara's comment, but felt too feeble to respond. "Amazing. She has a complete-light-spectrum aura, yet the blue hue for sadness is thickest," the Ara continued.

"Is it safe to take her into the Kingdom?" the Imaj asked.

"Yes," the Ara responded.

"Human, we are from the Kingdom of Norefole," the Imaj

said. "Our King requests your presence at the palace."

"The King?" she asked with hope in her eyes, though still cautious about whether these strangers were a threat to her.

"The ruler of Norefole, and he wishes to meet you," the Imaj said. Jill noticed how the Imaj cocked his head to the side, staring at the boulder she partially covered.

Imajs were highly skilled at finding images embedded within nature's tapestry, and could see what others could not. What appeared as random blemishes on a rock became objects to an Imaj, and this one observed a majestic lily on the boulder's surface. The Imaj leaned into the boulder and removed the fresh-cut flower, scent and all, and presented it to Jill. The extraction left only a slight indentation and wrinkle at the exact spot where the lily had been. Jill brushed her hand across the indentation in awe and bewilderment. Witnessing such mystery rejuvenated Jill. She had a hunch there was more magic beyond the Kingdom's walls, and that some might be potent enough to rescue her friends and return them all home. The Clades guided Jill from the outskirts of the Kingdom toward the palace. She contemplated telling them about the cone in her pocket, but decided to wait until she met the King.

The Kingdom had been carved from a massive mountain range, much taller than the one in Vesumio Valley. The King's majestic palace sat on the flat top of one of the core's middle mountains. The nearby mountains also had wide bands, which made them look like cinnamon rolls from above, and each band's perimeter had stone architecture on both sides, with an egress at each marketplace or residence. Grander and steeper mountains provided the full backdrop to the Kingdom.

The three approached the massive gate at the base of the mountain that housed the fortress-like palace and its series of sharply pointed towers, posted at each corner. They briskly passed by a few unarmed, but fully uniformed, soldiers.

"What are you?" Jill asked her traveling companions politely.

"We are Clades," the Ara responded. "I am of the Ara Clade and he is of the Imaj. You will meet other Clades inside. Come, the King awaits."

The interior of the Kingdom was a feast for the senses, with vertical flags of brilliant purple with distinct symbols, beings of different civilizations, the sounds of a bustling marketplace, and the smells of savory cooking. Jill's senses neared their combustion point. Instinctively, she knew she was safe within the Kingdom's walls.

The homes within the Kingdom ranged between two and five stories, with tall ceilings on each level. The front of the homes had two windows as wide as the doorway, positioned halfway up each side of the entrance. The homes were laid out in a spiral that followed the mountain's natural slant toward its pinnacle.

As they walked toward the palace, all who laid eyes upon them greeted them with a nod. Everyone looked upon Jill as if a puppy had been brought to a remote island. When they finally reached the top of the mountain, the Ara and Imaj were met by a Genet, who spoke to them in a tongue Jill didn't recognize. Jill left their side and walked to the far side of the plateau. She opened her arms wide to feel the sensational breeze passing through an iconic vista of the Kingdom and beyond. She greatly missed her friends, now more than ever.

"Come, we are about to start," the Ara said to Jill, directing her to come inside the palace.

Each tower held a different kind of room, and nearly all the towers were connected through tunnels at the plateau's base, in true labyrinth form. Heading into one of the east tower's six entrances, they beheld the full interior façade, which contained an elaborate grid of sparkling, blue-and-green jewels. Copper-colored Norefolian inscriptions danced above the surface of the walls, as if suspended in mid-air. Sometimes the words, appearing like they had a life of their own, turned hazy, then scattered and regrouped. Interspersed among the grid of jewels were strategically placed, narrow windows that allowed the outside elements to enter. Elongated, whimsically curved floating glass vases were set against the walls throughout the room. They resembled cascading waterfalls that spouted from the walls. The vases held bouquets of fresh and multicolored flowers, and each petal gave off a delicate, firefly-like light. Each arrangement emitted the brightness of a thick candle.

At the center of the room was a titanium, Z-shaped table that sat atop an oversized, plush, crimson rug. Spread on top of the table were five ornate stones bearing imprints of the same symbols as the flags outside. Clustered together nearby were three twenty-foot rock sculptures of previous Norefolian Kings, covered in cooled lava. Each tower held a different kind of room, and nearly all the towers were connected through tunnels at the plateau's base, in true labyrinth form.

The heads of each of the four Clades—the head Ara, A'riela; the head Loomer, Al'Visca; the head Genet, O'tis; and the head Imaj, I'pek—sat at the table. The fifth door opened, and the King entered, led by uniformed soldiers. "I have been waiting for you," the King said, looking directly at Jill.

"Me?" she said shyly.

"You were brave to enter Barren Woods, and fortunate not to have been encapsulated by the Cone Witch," said the King, who had famous telepathic powers and occasional premonitions of the future. The head Clades gaped at Jill, surprised that a single human could escape that environment unharmed. The King sat down at one end of the table, while Jill sat at the opposite end.

"Why do you think you were spared?" the King asked.

"Show us the other life you carry with you," O'tis said.

Jill then took the cone from her pocket and explained how she had used it to escape from the Witch. The King was very interested in the cone, as he had never seen one like it before. Jill passed it to the Ara sitting closest to her. "This is a seed of the Cone Witch," the Ara said, observing its emanating gray aura. "It must be calling for her."

The cone was then passed to the Genet. "This will be an exact replica of the Cone Witch," he said.

"Once we plant the cone within the Five Clades Garden, the Witch will be forced to enter the Kingdom's walls," the King said. "The temptation of germinating her own seedling will be too great to overcome."

The Norefolians deliberated on how to capture the Witch once she entered the Kingdom. Then Jill, barely able to contain herself, interrupted. "Please! Please! This cone helped me escape, and it might be exactly what you need to capture the Witch. But first, please help me get my friends back." Jill explained how the Witch had told her that she'd transformed Peet and Ray, how the Mocoons had taken Marilyn, and how the Grommels were now searching for her.

"The Witch is weakest if we extract her from the woods," the Imaj said. "Now, through this cone, you have found a way to bring her to us. Jill, if your friends were caught by the Cone Witch, they will stay dormant for a period of three days. It takes that long for her prey to transform permanently into a tree."

"I didn't want to believer her," Jill said.

"She lurks in those woods, feeding from them endlessly. She has the power to encapsulate life and transform it into a barren tree," the Imaj continued. "And only she can germinate her seedlings, one generation at a time."

"Now we must prepare, because the Cone Witch will not come alone," the King said. "She will use the Elicitors to enter. The entire Kingdom will soon be in jeopardy."

Knowing the Genets were like bloodhounds when it came to locating energy in all its forms, the King turned to O'tis and asked, "How difficult would it be to locate the two missing humans within Barren Woods?"

"Their energies should not be hard to distinguish, especially

82

since they were just transformed and are fresh to the decaying woods," O'tis responded.

"So their energies will come from inside those trees?" Jill asked.

"Yes, we Genets will be able to sense their energies," O'tis said.

"And we Imajs will be able to pull them out," I'pek said.

"I'd like to come too," Jill said.

"Very well then," the pensive King said. He ordered a small group of Clades to assemble and prepare for the rescue mission into Barren Woods. They each wore a weightless, silver-hooded cloak that kept the wearer's body temperature perfect. The group—O'tis, I'pek, twenty-four Genets, twelve Imajs, three Loomers, two Aras, and Jill—began the dangerous trek to Barren Woods.

* * *

When they reached Barren Woods, the Clades felt their powers becoming greatly diluted almost immediately, as fog and chill blanketed the woods. The Loomers disengaged from their bodies and proceeded to loom and weave through the extensive woods. The Genets struggled to sense the energies within the trees, as they searched for a very distinct, human energy. The Imajs saw outlines of creatures on the surface of the trees' bark, but most were faint because they had been decomposing for a long time.

Jill led the others to the area in the woods where her body had felt the stiffening effects of the Witch's powers. She and the two Aras stayed in that spot as markers while the others continued ahead. As the Clade group approached the core of the woods, the Genets sensed a tree with an intense energy unique from all the rest. The Imajs, except for I'Pek, moved onward while some of the Genets surrounded the tree. They lifted their heads up so their chins faced the tree, and extended their arms toward each other so that the inside of the forearms faced the same way. The Genets were all connected, their circle containing the radiating energy from the tree. Like a sculptor at work, I'pek pierced and peeled back the elaborate patterns of the bark until he could extract Peet. O'tis and I'pek swiftly guided a groggy Peet back toward Jill and the Aras. The Genets had found the tree quickly because Peet still had the chisel from the Regal Deer in his pocket, and they could easily sense its energy.

The Genets were about to disperse when, suddenly, the Witch sent a series of frigid gusts across the woods toward the Genet group, disabling their powers. The Genets could no longer detect the energies slowly percolating around them. The Witch had brought a large army of Elicitors with her, believing Jill and the Clades would soon return for the two children. The Elicitors made a surprise attack, surrounding the group and taking the Genets' powers, leaving them stranded and weak on the forest floor. The Witch strode through the fallen Genets and quickly converted them into barren trees.

The head Elicitor, Mangar, stayed behind with two young

Elicitors to observe the Witch's performance, while the other Elicitors moved ahead to comb the woods for more Clade powers. In the distance, three Loomers saw a group of Imajs heading straight into the army of Elicitors and tried to warn them, but it was too late. The Imajs could not materialize any objects in time to fight or escape. With their greater numbers, the Elicitors squelched their powers with ease. Two Loomers managed to sweep two of the Imajs out of harm's way, barely escaping to the outskirts of the woods. The third Loomer, however, failed to escape, giving the Elicitors three kinds of Clade powers that day. The Cone Witch zoomed to the fallen Imajs and transformed them into barren trees as she had the Genets. "And to think there are many more Genets and Imajs within the Kingdom," the Witch said, proud of her new additions.

After the Witch transformed the Imajs, Mangar and the two young Elicitors traveled in the opposite direction to search for other intruders. One of the young Elicitors spotted a human and the two Aras. They appeared defenseless, standing alone in the Witch's woods. It was too easy, thought the overzealous young Elicitors. Mangar ordered the young Elicitors to watch them from afar. But when Mangar left, they snuck up on the Aras. Immediately, the Aras produced exquisite aura bands, shields of dancing color, and Jill stood behind them.

The young Elicitors thirsted for the ability to create an aura band, but even the youngest of Elicitors knew they could not elicit another Clade's powers while the power was being wielded. These Elicitors had heard of such bands, but had never personally witnessed the power in use. The two mesmerized Elicitors lusted for such exquisite ability, and decided to attempt to take those powers anyway. When they closed in, however, Jill made a most unusual howling sound. The Elicitors were startled by the noise. Even the Aras' protective bands dipped slightly to the floor from the howling.

"Try to elicit that sound from her," one Elicitor told the other.

"No way, I'd rather weave aura bands any day," the other responded.

Jill's howl had momentarily distracted all the Clades within listening distance, and was distinct enough to make Peet turn in her direction. He headed toward her, with I'pek and O'tis following.

"There is one Ara for each of us," the young Elicitor said.

"Yes, but I want..." the other began.

O'tis had now picked up the young Elicitors' energies and led the charge toward them. The Elicitors ran off, knowing they stood no chance of eliciting the powers of the head Clades. Once the group had reunited, O'tis urged all of them to leave the woods and head home while he continued searching for the others. O'tis then disappeared back into the woods.

When O'tis finally reached the Imajs, fewer than a quarter remained untransformed. To his horror, he witnessed an Elicitor ripping away the powers from the last fallen Imaj before the Witch transformed him into a barren tree. O'tis knew he had to avoid being captured; the Kingdom could not afford to have the

Witch gain the powers of a head Clade. There was nothing he could do but retreat for the sake of the Kingdom.

O'tis was heading back to the Kingdom when he felt a familiar energy nearby. It was I'pek. "My friend, I was too late," O'tis reported. "They were nearly all encapsulated when I arrived, and there were too many Elicitors to fight alone. Did the humans make it out of the woods safely?"

"Yes, but one still remains," I'pek said.

"We'll soon return with greater forces, but we must leave now before we expose the entire Kingdom to danger," O'tis said.

"Agreed," I'pek said. They trekked out together, bobbing and weaving through hundreds of trees, when I'pek suddenly stopped before a tree. He had noticed the familiar image of a legendary Grommel on the bark of one of the trees.

Peet, Jill, and the Aras had decided to wait near the outskirts of the woods, despite O'tis's direction to continue toward the Kingdom. A short while later, I'pek and O'tis appeared, along with a Grommel who had a distinctive brown spot. "Gromyko!" Peet yelled as he came out from hiding behind a boulder.

"My dear friend from Barrenville, and his tent builder friend; you are here," Gromyko said as he brushed up against Peet, then Jill. "I have not forgotten you."

"Where have you been all this time?" Peet asked.

"The Cone Witch encapsulated me soon after I left Barrenville, but the worst is yet to come. We are all in grave danger. While encapsulated within the tree, I overheard Mangar and the Witch scheming to invade the Kingdom tonight, to reclaim a seedling of hers. We must alert the King and the Grommel battalion!"

As the group swiftly gained distance from the woods, Gromyko asked Peet and Jill how they'd come to meet again here in Barren Woods. Peet filled Gromyko in on the highlights of their journey, including the disappearances of Marilyn and Ray. Gromyko was deeply saddened and had many more questions for him, but there wasn't time to waste. The two Loomers who had rescued the Imajs dropped them off near a boulder ahead, where the Loomers had left their bodies. Gromyko made his special call for his desert lizard, and the statuesque lizard arrived within minutes. Gromyko mounted and headed back to Grommel Lake without incident. The Clades and children, each wearing light cloaks, moved swiftly across the land from Barren Woods to the Kingdom.

*   *   *

Since the search for Marilyn and Gromyko began, guards had been posted at each side of Grommel Lake's entrance. Upon spotting Gromyko, the guards sounded the horn, and Grommels quickly gathered at the front entrance. Gromyko was greeted by all, including his family and his commander, Grog.

"Gromyko, we've been searching for you throughout the deserts," Grog said. "We've looked everywhere. Why did you not return to us after your journey to Barrenville?"

Gromyko explained how, after he discovered Marilyn had

opened the capillary, he used it as a way to lure the Mocoon away from Barrenville. When he jumped into the capillary, however, its strong suction pulled him all the way through until he landed on a bed of tall, spiny plants that immobilized him. He had arrived somewhere on the outskirts of Vesumio Valley in Plain Desert, far from Grommel Lake. The Mocoon soon fell right on top of him. Because its mass was made of sand wafers, it did not physically harm him, but it took him prisoner. "The Mocoon took me directly to Barren Woods on a sand sled. When we arrived, the Cone Witch was waiting to interrogate me about the Ascentia. When I would not speak, she encapsulated me."

As he looked at his fellow Grommels, he felt for the first time like a foreigner among his own kind. He had lived away from home longer than he'd lived at Grommel Lake. He had traveled more extensively than any other Grommel, through the many terrains of Norefole and the many biomes of Earth. Through his duties, he had encountered the various and unique inhabitants of each place, and had become a truly universal Grommel.

Before the other Grommels could ask him any more questions, Gromyko warned them about the Witch's plan to invade the Kingdom that very evening. Grog immediately ordered the battalion of Grommels to make ready for battle. Although not all Grommels fought, each had a customary duty to perform, and so all began to prepare. The Grommels' gurgling throat sounds, a sound declaring battle, echoed throughout Grommel Lake like the roar of a coliseum.

Grayle, who had been standing silently near Gromyko, told

him, "Before you run off to join the battalion again, tell me how you've been. Come, I'll walk with you." He nodded, awkwardly smiling at her.

"Things seem different here," Gromyko said.

"You've just been away from home for a long time," she said, happy to see him. "It's so good to lay eyes on you again." Gromyko realized how she had always been a constant support in his life. He enjoyed her companionship, as she was sweet and pure hearted, and had a calming nature about her. As they approached his cavern, he accidentally stumbled from tiredness, and grabbed her shoulder. He felt his elbow shake and his heart race. All he had the courage to do was to pat her shoulder and tell her they'd catch up later. He walked on and leaped straight up to his cavern above.

While the Grommels organized, Peet, Jill, and the others reached the Kingdom. They soon met with the other head Clades and the King. They confirmed that the Cone Witch would come that night and that she would not arrive alone. "It was almost too late for Gromyko, had you not released him from the tree today," the King said. "When you did that, I read his unrested thoughts about what he overheard between the Witch and Mangar."

*   *   *

The Witch furiously paced herself three feet into the ground while she brainstormed how to reclaim her seedling, a future Witch, from within the Kingdom's walls. The Witch was already in a foul mood, as she had been recovering from the collarbone injury that nearly caused her demise. She had not tried to transport again since her trip to Barrenville in search of the Regal Deer, fearing that the gravitational pull of the aerial bridges might cause her collarbone to fracture.

"Your Highness," Mangar said. "The boy and the Grommel have escaped from the woods."

"You fool!" the Witch yelled. "It was your job to capture new life and, at the very least, preserve all of my trees!"

"I understand. It was my error. However, some of our Clade now temporarily have the powers of the Imajs and Genets. The Clades who hold these new powers, through my alliance, are now part of your collection, Your Highness. We just need the Regal Deer to make them permanent," Mangar said.

"Yes, but there are not enough Elicitors filled with other Clade powers yet. I want all of you to carry their powers so you'll never have to elicit from them again. Now, get me the Loomer!" she said, recalling the young Loomer being held prisoner at Plain Desert by her Mocoons. "Mature Clade or not, we'll have to make use of him, although his powers may not be stable. Let's see how much of the army we can push through him."

The Witch knew she would require a Loomer's power in her quest to enter the Kingdom. She and Mangar had spent countless hours deliberating and strategizing about ways to defeat the other Clades and the King, and install her as the Queen of Norefole.

"Ah, but there is more news, Your Highness." Mangar said. "We also captured a mature Loomer today."

"Get ready to travel, then. Our time has come. My seedling calls for me."

*   *   *

Marilyn and the Loomer named Al'Bual continued to contemplate ways to escape their desert prison.

"I wish we had an Imaj here to create a visual so we could travel to it and escape this hot desert," Al'Bual said. "The Mocoons have starved me of visuals, so that I won't expel my energy and get help. It's not easy being a young Loomer because we need concrete visuals to loom, and my powers don't always do what I want when I try to use them."

"Maybe I can create a visual," Marilyn said, realizing she still had the two droplets from the pods in the desert cradles. "I can use the dyes from the pods to color the sand."

"How? You are not an Imaj."

"I can color us into an oasis. I've colored lots of times while Peet was out gathering specimens for his jars. You'll see." As she placed the droplet in her mouth, she conjured up a pile of steamed spinach in her mind, and spit it out on the sand. "We have green now," she said proudly, watching the spinach clump with the sand. She quickly outlined a palm tree in the sand with her finger. Al'Bual just raised his eyebrows in curiosity as he watched Marilyn draw.

"We need brown quickly," he stated, realizing that an image was forming.

"Easy," she said. "Chocolate." She conjured up a milk-chocolate bar in her mind, placed the second droplet in her mouth, and spit out liquid chocolate on the sand. "Chocolate and spinach are quite nice together," she said as she drew the tree trunks.

Al'Bual was surprised by the little human, and he could sense his power reviving. As soon as Marilyn placed the final strokes on the image on the ground, the Loomer reached for Marilyn's hand. He expelled his energy into the form of his body and transported them both to an oasis outside of Plain Desert. "I did it!" he proudly told her, still dizzy from using his powers.

"There it is! There is my home, the Kingdom."

"Where?" she asked, still rubbing sand out of her eyes. She turned and looked up. Marilyn was awed by the unrivaled beauty of the majestic Kingdom. "What's that fire in all the corners of that mountain?"

Al'Bual regained his composure and saw the fires lit over the palace, which he explained was a signal that the Kingdom was in danger and an enemy was approaching. He tried to transport Marilyn inside the Kingdom's walls, but his energy became erratic and unstable. He loomed ahead in a jagged line, as she walked in the direction of the Kingdom.

CHAPTER TEN

THE BATTLE AT
FIVE CLADES GARDEN

The vast Five Clades Garden had the shape of a giant eye, with a central circle surrounded by greenery that was heavily textured like an English garden. The Witch planned to invade the garden by first sending Mangar, disguised as her in a black, slate-textured, hooded cloak. It was an ingenious plan, as the Witch knew the King and the Clades would never expect an Elicitor to enter the Kingdom through the garden. She counted on at least one of the other Clades would use their powers upon seeing the Elicitor; young Clades, especially, had difficulty controlling the exertion of their powers. First, however, the Witch would have Mangar take the powers of another Elicitor—an ability only he possessed as the head of his Clade; this would amplify his own powers twice over.

As planned, Mangar entered the Five Clades Garden and walked through it unimpeded. The palace surroundings were still and quiet. Unbeknown to Mangar, the heads of the other four Clades were stationed at the four corners of the garden, with groups of their respective Clades behind them. The Aras tried to penetrate his cloak to determine the characteristics or quality of his aura, but they could not, making them watch the cloaked being more closely.

The King, through a premonition, had seen the Witch's presence in the garden and thought it natural for her to enter the garden fields in search of her seedling. He and the other Clades expected the Elicitors to break in through the labyrinth tunnels, so many of the Genets were stationed at the entranceways of those tunnels around the base of the mountain, waiting to sense the Elicitor energies and warn the others.

Mangar appeared as a silhouette in the garden and passed by Peet and Jill, who were secretly tucked near the garden walls. Like the others, Jill thought this being was the Witch but, when she noticed that the collarbone was not fractured, she hollered, "She's an imposter! That's not the Witch!" The Elicitor, in one swoop, uncloaked and revealed his true self. The head Clades tried to move away from the garden, knowing their own strengths could be used against the others on behalf of the Witch. Mangar targeted A'riela, who was closest to him, and swiftly elicited all of her Ara powers, leaving her near death. The young Clades could barely resist releasing their powers around a head Elicitor, especially since he had amplified his own. They stepped further back in their groups, not understanding what was happening to them.

Mangar immediately used A'riela's power to create an aura band around the garden to shield the other Elicitors as they entered. The band he projected was black, an ominous color never produced by an Ara. Using the power of the recently captured Loomer, the other Elicitors sprouted from the garden one at a time, until the entire Elicitor Clade had entered the Kingdom. The Witch followed stealthily, shadowing an Elicitor's energy until they surfaced. Upon her arrival, she created a fog that lowered the temperature of the garden and surrounding area. She appeared to float over the garden to collect the seedling, then placed it inside her cone shell. Once Mangar saw the Cone Witch, the last to arrive, he released the band.

The Elicitors, although well outnumbered, descended on their fellow Clades, eliciting powers at will. The Witch, using the fog through which only she could navigate, quickly targeted the remaining head Clades and converted them into barren trees. With the head Clades gone, chaos ruled the others. It was open season as the Elicitors feverishly hunted the other Clades for their powers. "It feels good to be back home, doesn't it?" Mangar said to the other Elicitors as they walked around him.

Although their energy-spotting sensors were now weakened, the Genets gathered as many young Clades as they could and directed them toward the Aras. The Loomers also swept as many

96

young to safety as they could find. Very young Clades could be destroyed easily because their powers were still developing, making them far more vulnerable. The Aras who had not yet been elicited encircled the other remaining Clades. Each Ara, however, could enclose only a few non-Aras at a time within their protective bands. The Imajs also dispersed quickly and headed toward the palace towers, which led to the tunnels beneath and was where they secretly kept their combat slates. These slates, with infinite designs, were used to create and materialize objects. But only a few Imajs reached them in time.

Four Aras surrounded the King, Peet, Jill, and the young Clades, forming quadrants of protective clusters. One of the elder Aras placed Jill between the four clusters of bands. Jill felt a sensational dizziness as the Aras near her used their auras to weave impenetrable shields of bands. The static-like buzz of the Elicitors taking powers from the other Clades drowned out most other sound. As long as the Clades continuously used their powers, however, the Elicitors could not extract them. That meant the other Clades had to stay in continual motion when utilizing their powers, as even a slight break could make them fall victim to an Elicitor. Many of those who released their powers to aid others were also elicited.

Nearly all the Loomers dislodged their energies from their bodies, so the Elicitors could not extract their powers. Several Loomers were able to transport Imajs to their prefabricated slates near the towers to conceive a new plan. Many Elicitors pursued the Loomers' energy masses, while other Elicitors waited near their physical bodies for their return. Knowing that Elicitors found Loomer powers the most desirable, the remaining Genets stationed themselves near the Loomers' bodies, to try to stop the Elicitors from taking their powers.

The Elicitors were fully engaged in combat and soon most had taken powers, leaving the other Clades temporarily depleted. Then a small group of Loomers, along with Imajs holding slates, reappeared near the garden. Once on the ground, the Imajs materialized prefabricated doors in strategic locations, through which their fellow Clades could escape.

"You have a choice to return, to rejoin the sphere and the Kingdom," the King told Mangar telepathically. "Stop what you are doing... in the memory of your ancestors."

"I pleaded with you to help change us, but you denied us," Mangar responded. "The Witch will soon take your place, and our kind, filled with all five powers, will be able to sustain the sphere alone. You've already sacrificed the sphere by letting us leave the Kingdom." He then directed several Elicitors toward the Aras' bands protecting the King, young Clades, and humans. The Elicitors made several attempts to penetrate the bands, but could not break them. Still, they knew it would only be a matter of time.

The King watched helplessly as the Elicitors infused themselves with their fellow Clades' powers, violently ripping them away before the Witch transformed many of the fallen Clades into barren trees. As the Elicitors took over the Kingdom, the Witch diffused the fog. Suddenly, the King, through his premonition, got a glimpse of steadfast Grommels heading toward the Kingdom. The King communicated telepathically to Grog that the Clades were tiring and falling quickly. "It may be too late," the King whispered under his breath. Those encircled by the Aras despaired over the others outside the bands. The Aras' protective bands were weakening, so those inside would have to be ready for when the Aras could no longer hold up the bands. As more of the Clades fell, fewer and fewer bands were seen throughout the grounds.

"Get ready to run, my young Clades," an Ara said to those within her protective band. "The doorway is straight ahead. Don't look back. Just keep running. Ready?"

Some of them had never seen an Elicitor before and they were scared. The band dissipated. The Ara and a couple of Genets nearby charged the approaching Elicitors, to ensure the youngsters made it through the doorway. The Ara was the first to be elicited and transformed into a barren tree.

Then the land began to thunder and rattle. From a distance, coming up the mountain, emerald jewels sparkled at the palace gates. The battalion of armored Grommels had arrived, riding on their lizards. The Grommels wore belts and spiked, armored helmets. They tore across the grounds to hunt down the Elicitors scattered throughout the Kingdom. Upon nearing the garden, they dismounted to avoid hitting the newly created barren trees. The Grommels, with their light-studded eyes, could momentarily blind anyone who saw them. Once within range of the Elicitors, the Grommels launched quill-like slivers into them. The slivers interrupted the eliciting process, reverting the powers back to their rightful Clades.

In the far distance, the Grommels could see four clusters of elaborate, multi-colored bands rotating around the King, Peet, and others. The Cone Witch also noticed the unusual movement and colors of the elaborate, circular bands. She promptly recognized both of the children who had escaped from Barren Woods. No one before them had ever escaped after being encapsulated, not even any of the Clades. Perhaps, she thought, these two humans had proven that they had special powers. She was determined not to leave without the humans now, and the King quickly realized what she wanted. Without further delay, she directed Mangar to attend to the elaborate aura bands himself. Mangar slowly approached the band encircling the King.

Just then, Marilyn arrived at the palace gate shadowing Al'Bual's energy. A Loomer approached the two and pleaded with them to hide in the labyrinth. The Loomer picked up Marilyn, but she refused to hide when she saw Peet and Jill in the distance. She yelled her brother's name, "Peet! Peet!" The Loomer released her and, when she landed on the ground, she saw Elicitors taking powers and hurting the others. Several Elicitors standing nearest the entrance gates saw the scuffle between Marilyn and the two Loomers and headed toward them.

The Loomer again attempted to lead Marilyn and Al'Bual to safety, but it was too late. Marilyn next watched the struggle between two Elicitors with Loomer powers and the two Loomers. They wrestled high in the sky in acrobatic ways she had never seen before. Three more Elicitors approached and Marilyn now stood alone among them, a predicament she had faced before. This time, her short temper got the best of her. She clenched her fists, stood tall to lengthen herself, puffed out her chest, pushed her arms out, and looked upon them with a deadly stare. Then, with clarity and might, she yelled, "Stop!" The three Elicitors surrounding her became suspended immediately.

Marilyn, realizing she had somehow pushed the Elicitors away without touching them, felt inspired. She wondered why she did not have this power before, when the Cone Witch and Elicitors had appeared to her in Plain Desert. Several more Elicitors approached her. Marilyn again yelled for them to stop, and again pushed her arms out until they were fully extended, just as she had seen the Elicitors do when taking powers. Like the others, those Elicitors were immediately suspended in action. The Norefolians and the humans alike were amazed to see the young human was capable of handling the stealthy Elicitors. Marilyn, now feeling completely untouchable, started walking alone in the direction of the elaborate band to meet her brother and Jill.

The Witch also observed Marilyn's performance at the entrance. "Enough!" she yelled. "I see I must do things myself." She headed toward Marilyn, boldly and with malice. Mangar and the Elicitors nearest him turned to watch the Witch.

Peet demanded to be released from the protective band to get his sister but, for his own safety and the safety of the others, the Ara would not stop the stream of bands from encircling the group. The King telepathically directed the Grommels closest to the human at the entrance to surround her. Now each time an Elicitor attempted to draw out Marilyn's powers, the Grommels shot slivers to stop them. The Grommels were not clear what power they were protecting, but the Elicitors craved it.

"Maybe I can use this now!" Peet excitedly told the King, pulling the chisel out of his pocket. "The Witch suffered a broken collarbone when she transformed the Regal Deer into the Whimsical Tree, and this is part of that deer."

"Well, it might just buy us some time," the King said. He directed the Ara protecting Peet and a young Imaj to release the band. Peet sprinted toward Marilyn. A'ya, the Ara who was encircling the King, released her band at the same time. The King stepped next to the young Imaj, and they were encircled together. A'ya then caught up to Peet and encircled him while they ran together toward Marilyn.

While Gromyko shot slivers at Elicitors, he heard Peet's faint voice over all the chaos. He then turned to search for Peet and the Witch. As Peet and A'ya approached Gromyko, he yelled for Peet to throw him the chisel. When Peet raised his arm to throw it, A'ya released her power, realizing his intention when she saw Gromyko nearby. Gromyko caught the chisel, then leapt high into the air to get an aerial perspective of the battleground. With the chisel in his belt, Gromyko leapt in a fury toward the Witch. The King next telepathically next directed the Grommels nearest the Witch to surround Gromyko as he rampaged toward her. A sudden swarm of white bodies ascended over the Elicitors and toward Gromyko, who hid within it as he approached the Witch.

He took one last leap, strongly clutching the chisel. Gromyko collided forcefully with the Witch, and pierced the scales of her cone-shelled figure. She gasped for air.

The Witch had not expected the Regal Deer's marrow to be an antidote to her power. Because she had twice encapsulated the chisel and its power—once in Barrenville and once in Barren Woods—she had tainted the marrow within the chisel and made it toxic to her own body. When Gromyko pierced the skin beneath her cone shell, the chisel triggered a process of over-fertilization, causing her veins to gradually disintegrate. The cone scales around the puncture wound started to shed, and her body suddenly weakened, nearly dropping the seedling from her cone shell.

The Elicitors looked around at each other, unsure of what to do next. Rather than pursue the King, Mangar told the Elicitors fall back, with or without any elicited powers. Mangar also ordered two Elicitors, who had gained Loomer powers, to carry the Witch away from the Kingdom. The other Elicitors promptly followed them as they retreated from the palace, leaving a devastated Five Clades Garden behind. The Clades who remained used their powers to search for one another.

Peet, Jill, and Marilyn found their way to each other and embraced. "We must return to Barren Woods to rescue Ray," Jill said.

The King approached them with a heavy heart. "There are also many Norefolians to untomb, both here and in Barren Woods," the King said. The children looked at him quizzically, curious as to how he had heard their conversation. The Imajs, skilled in the delicate process of extraction, worked quickly to first untomb those within the palace. A small group was already slowly gathering at the Kingdom's gates for another rescue mission in Barren Woods.

"The Witch, if she lives, will likely retreat to the desert," the King said. "If she returns to Barren Woods, she will be too exposed, knowing we will be heading there next to save those we can."

CHAPTER ELEVEN

NEW BEGINNINGS

As the Imajs entered Barren Woods without the obstruction of fog or cold, they easily found a notable transparency in the markings on many of the trees. If a barren tree's bark had no depth in its markings, then it was a permanent tree and the encapsulated life was lost. Otherwise, the body within was still alive. Imajs scanned countless permanent trees, noting that the beings entombed within were slowly expiring.

Within the trees were the bodies of Grommels, Clades, other Norefolian species, and, of course, Ray. All had been captured over time, and for most of them it was too late for rescue. The Witch had encapsulated their living bodies to provide a source of ongoing fertilization for her woods, and she made sure they never went hungry.

After the Imajs left for the woods, the King turned to Peet, Jill, Marilyn, and Gromyko. "Norefole experiences more lunar and solar eclipses than Earth. An eclipse occurs tonight, and an Ara will be born," he said.

Gromyko handed the chisel back to Peet. "This rightfully belongs to you," he said.

The expecting Ara father joined them and addressed Peet, Jill, and Marilyn. "You are the first humans who have traveled here and bonded with Norefolians. It would be an honor to have all of you meet our newest Clade. Come. You must stay for a true Norefolian celebration. Tonight new life, once again, will take hold on these lands."

They happily agreed and headed inside the palace to one of the tower's formal sitting rooms. "Where did you get your powers?" Peet asked his sister.

"I don't know," Marilyn said, "but I like it."

"Norefole is a place where the purity of all life forms resonates," the expecting Ara father said. "In order to survive, Marilyn was driven to mimic powers she had witnessed. She also appears to have a strong, rebellious personality. She was able to ward off the Elicitors because she accessed a source of power within that wasn't available to her outside of Norefole, or without exposure to the five Clade powers."

"Your experiences in Norefole will serve as the foundation to find your ancestral power—your core energy, which is already within your lineage fiber," the King said. "When you arrive home, the Stewards will help you access and awaken this forgotten power."

"Mastive told us the Stewards are the Council back home," Jill said. "Who are they really?"

"They are from the land of Tortel, several nights' journey from here," Gromyko said. "They are builders and educators by nature. They resemble your kind, and a select few have traveled to your world almost as frequently as some of us Grommels."

"The Stewards will guide you to learn more about what you have seen and experienced here," the King said. "It won't make sense to you now, but I promise it will soon. As for your friend, he was not exposed to the Clade powers like you three were, so we cannot speak to him of what Marilyn did here today. It is best for everyone this way."

Peet turned to Jill and Marilyn sitting beside him, and said. "We must also promise never to reveal the Clade powers to our parents, or anyone else back home. They'll never understand." They quickly agreed.

The whole Kingdom eagerly awaited the birth of the new Ara, as well as the return of Ray and the others who had been encapsulated by the Cone Witch. Norefolians worked in an orderly fashion, tending to the details of the festivities. They decorated the entire palace with the national Norefolian orchids. Unique flowers with long, rope-like stems, they stood upright and wavered in the breeze like living coral in seawater. Norefolians unraveled the orchids from the top of the fortress walls and let them cascade down the mountain. Because of the orchids' length and flowing movement, few were needed to drape the palace or its mountainsides. The palace grounds were also adorned with orange blossoms, the symbol of renewal. As one walked over them, pressing down on the petals, they infused the air with a familiar fragrance of fresh citrus.

To prepare for the evening's ceremony, the children had each been given one of the numerous private guest rooms of the King's quarters. The doors on their rooms had inscriptions of an unusual symbol, in which the insignias of each Clade were superimposed atop one another to form the shape of an eye. The Aras' insignia was a circular band, the Genets' an oval field, the Elicitors' a thunderbolt, the Loomers' a wrinkled thread, and the Imajs' a blot speck. Inside the guest rooms, the same symbol appeared embossed on a heavy, square glass near a carafe of water at each bedside table. The symbol, along with the words "Ancestral Powers," was also engraved on octagonal, thin, slate pendants left for each of them.

Once the children were ready, each wearing the special pendant and waiting outside their room, they were escorted to an atrium at the center of their floor. They leaned over the rails to view the floors below and above their own, and saw many other guests doing the same. The ceiling had a dome made of multicolored glass, which rippled like water when light moved across it. The walls along the wide stairwell were covered by streaming murals of a moving sky, similar to those in the acorn pods drawn by Mastive. The children lined up at the staircase and headed down. With each step they took, it was easier to imagine moving through the sky.

Once at the bottom of the staircase, the three of them were guided outside the King's quarters to the courtyard within the palace, where they were to dine with the King that evening. The head Clades were already gathered there, along with their immediate families, part of the Grommel battalion, and the full family of the soon-to-arrive Ara. The festivities were a joyous time.

Inside the palace's master kitchen, an orderly team of cooks, bakers, and other food preparers worked at a feverish pace. Outside the nearest kitchen's entrance was a V-formation of culinary stations, formed by two rows at each angle. The rest of the tables fanned out in rows around them. Each station had a pearl-white tent top adorned with a whimsical, flat-bronze design showing that station's offerings. At each of the ten stations, two gourmet chefs produced delectable, artistic cuisine. That evening, the entire Kingdom dined outdoors in the courtyard, overlooking the mountainous backdrop. Aromas of pumpkin muffins and cooked hens came from the kitchen, and the courtyard soon became a panorama of visual and edible delights.

Kites—designed, crafted, painted, and assembled by each Loomer Clade family—dotted the sky. Young Loomers floated in the sky, whizzing the kites around with their energy. The Genets created three life-sized rock sculptures, half covered with cooled-lava glaze, that greatly resembled Peet, Jill, and Marilyn. The Imajs extracted prehistoric fish fossils from the nearby mountains, and carved them out for table decor. The younger

Aras harvested Norefolian fruits from the garden and wove them into a band of beauty that circled overhead. These artistic works were some of the ways the Clades celebrated life.

As darkness fell over Norefole, the temperature remained comfortable, the sky was clear, and the heavens billowed with lustrous stars. The sky between the bright stars and the mountaintop was unforgettable. Toward the conclusion of their dinner, the search party returned with few survivors. Families were reunited, and Ray rejoined his friends. Peet, Jill, and Marilyn ran to him and embraced him. Tears of joy streamed down Ray's cheeks.

"Welcome Ray," the King said. "We've been waiting for you." The King then handed him a pendant identical to those of his friends. "I am fulfilled to see you all together, and I know there is a great deal to speak of between the four of you."

Grateful and overwhelmed, Ray thanked him for the pendant and for reuniting him with his friends. The children were very happy to be together once again and excited that they could now return home. The Clades and the King knew the children's time in Norefole was now limited.

For the next several hours, many of their conversations recounted the details of the battle with the Elicitors. After the feast, nearly everyone present gathered at the grand, candle-shaped fountain in the center of the courtyard and watched the lunar eclipse begin. As the moon's light was overshadowed, the horns sounded and the doors opened to one of the rooms within the King's quarters. An Ara had been born.

The King, A'riela, and the parents with their newborn stepped out of the room onto the long balcony protruding from the palace directly above the courtyard. Per tradition, the mother first handed the newborn to the King. In a procession, the King walked ahead of the three Aras, then placed the newborn Ara into the Golden Cradle, which was stationed like a podium at the end of the balcony. There was silence all around when A'riela and the King held their palms over the new Ara's chest. Then, from within the cradle, the newborn generated a tiny white band above himself, causing a wild outburst of cheers from below. The wind carried the cheers in every direction of the Kingdom.

The King next called for the humans to join him on the balcony, and they quickly ran into the King's quarters. "Ray, Jill, Marilyn, and Peet, you will always be referred to as the Ambassadors of the Human Race here in Norefole, and we are indebted to you," the King said. From the balcony, Ray noticed the three sculptures on the lawn were replicas of Jill, Marilyn, and Peet. "The pendants you each received are your reminders of Norefole and all that exists within," the King said as he waved his palm over each of the four children. "Let the festivities continue." More cheers came as the Clades formed a line near the King's quarters to greet the humans and congratulate the Aras.

*   *   *

The next morning back in Barrenville, Hady walked into the living room, expecting to find four sleeping children. Instead she

111

saw tossed blankets, pillows, board games, and wrappers they had left behind from their sleepover. She placed a pot of water on the stovetop, and began to clean up. As she reached down to organize the linens in the basket near the sofa, she glanced out the patio door. In dismay, she took a long pause. Hady was astonished to see the partially collapsed tent in the yard, a trail of sleeping bags and toys. Worse, thick veins of water had appeared overnight, cutting through the grasses like cracks in a cement sidewalk.

Hady stepped out on the patio to look around, and saw some of her neighbors were also studying the mysterious waterways. She walked onto the grass and followed a particularly plump vein of water to the end of her backyard. At random spots along the vein, she bent down to place her hand into the water. It was cold, but shallow enough that she could easily touch the ground underneath. Then she found a round hole that resembled a pond filled with water. It was the only round hole she found. She placed her hand into the pond and felt thick, rope-like roots on the bottom. Her heart raced as she wondered where the children had gone and what had happened. She withdrew her arm and dried herself with the wafting ends of her robe. "Peet, Marilyn, where are you? Ray? Jill?" But she got no answer. Hady yelled for the children repeatedly, but still there was no answer. She searched inside the house, but found no trace of them. It was not like her children to suddenly disappear.

When Marilyn had dug the pond for Gromyko, she punctured the virgin land of Barrenville in the heart of its native root system. This created a wrinkling in the land, starting with the ground closest to the pond. When the capillary finally dissolved, it sent water gushing up and out of the ground. The thick and fibrous root metropolis had captured and absorbed most of the water, but the overrun caused growing water veins that filled in the wrinkles. The always-growing roots had prevented a complete disaster by growing over the relatively small puncture, but another impact in the heart of Barrenville could trigger a larger-scale, devastating change to the land.

"Ansel! Ansel!" Hady screamed as she ran into her bedroom. From a dead sleep, Ansel sprang forward, alarmed. "The children are missing and water has seeped out all over the land," Hady exclaimed.

Ansel leapt out of bed and looked out the window facing the backyard. Worried and exasperated, he walked toward the patio to observe the damage. "How did this happen?" he wondered aloud, still waking up.

"Ansel, there is something you need to see," Hady said. She led him to the pond, and told him to touch the bundled root mass under the water. "There are grasses in the water veins, but not in this spot."

"Where are your digging tools?" he asked, now growing more concerned.

"They are in the shed," Hady responded. They both went to the shed and discovered the trowel had dirt on it, and so did the bottom of her garden canvas bag. Hady always cleaned her digging tools, the way an artist cleans her brushes, before putting them away.

"The children must have dug that pond here last night," Ansel said. "Perhaps that is what caused the cracks in the land. Now they're probably out exploring with their friends, following the water veins throughout the town. I'm sure they'll be back soon. But they'll have a lot of explaining to do." Ansel and Hady discretely searched the nearby properties for similar pools of water, but found none.

Within minutes, the Barrenville alarm went off, and the sound was deafening. Between the concern about the mysterious water veins and the ringing of the alarm, nearly the entire town assembled at the town hall in record time. Wanerhess Hoise and the full Council were gathered on a platform facing the growing crowd.

Once enough people had gathered, Wanerhess stepped up to the podium to speak. "A vital point in our root metropolis was punctured, and some of the native roots removed. The water veins on the ground will not expand, for now. The excess water collected overnight will slowly seep back into the ground. Thankfully, given the small size of the hole, our root metropolis was strong enough to heal itself. All permits for digging and excavation have been suspended indefinitely. It is very important that no one further disturb the town's land. We are responsible for much of the continent's stabilization. Any imbalance of land to water will not occur on my watch."

During his speech, Ansel and Hady felt like they themselves should seep into the ground, as they believed Wanerhess had identified exactly where the puncture had occurred. Eventually,

Ansel and Hady found Ray's and Jill's parents at the gathering. They had all been searching for one another, thinking the others knew where their children were. As the three sets of parents conferred, however, it became apparent that none of them knew where the children were. After Wanerhess finished his speech, he made his way through the crowd to the anxious parents. "It's important you come to Mera Lab this afternoon," he told them.

"Is it about our children?" Jill's mother asked.

"Yes," Wanerhess sternly replied. "They are alright and they're resting at Settlers' Hills from their extracurricular activities last night. The Council and I need to meet with you in private. Say, four this afternoon?" He walked past them before any of them could respond. The parents all felt responsible for the puncture and the resulting water damage.

"I thought they stayed at your home last night," Jill's father said to Ansel.

"Yes, they did," Ansel responded. "We last saw them watching a movie and playing board games in the living room. When we woke up this morning, they were gone."

*   *   *

The Council had gathered for an emergency meeting on the night the children entered Norefole. Wanerhess had promptly notified the Council members of the puncture and the tearing of the native roots, as well as the water gushing from the hole. He also gave them his assessment of the damage done to the dual-heart valve of the root metropolis. Neither the Council members nor Wanerhess slept that evening as they deliberated about how to mend the immediate damage to Barrenville.

At four in the afternoon, Wanerhess and the twelve Stewards who made up the full Council waited for the children's parents inside Mera Lab's conference room. Each set of parents drove up the long, winding road that led to the barn with silos on each side of its entrance, and to the adjacent Mera Lab. The farm's air had a fragrant grass smell, and the sound of grasshoppers could be heard all around. Jill's parents were the last to arrive. When Jill's mother got out of the car, a strong wind knocked her hat off her head. Jill's father, who walked with a cane, retrieved her hat from where it landed over on his side of the car. He closed the door behind him, and together they walked toward Mera Lab.

In addition to being a world-renowned laboratory, Mera Lab had a small public library and an exhibit gallery that illustrated the domes' crop production, so the facility was not unfamiliar to any of them. The building's corridors were partially lined with three-dimensional portraits of the moving prairie, and all the east-facing windows offered unobstructed views of the domes.

Jill's parents walked through security and were greeted by a receptionist, who sat near the main elevator to the tower's conference room. Once all the parents were present, they were directed to the elevator by the receptionist. "Let's take you up there now," she said to the group. "The Council is waiting."

As the parents entered the conference room, they were greeted by all the members of the Council. Hugh, the head of the

Council, spoke first. "As we speak, your children are being transported here from the other side of the farm. They are absolutely and solely responsible for compromising our root metropolis. In a single night, they punctured the ground, dug up native roots, and used tools of excavation without authorization. Generally, we would respond to such actions with a lawsuit on behalf of the town and the Council." Hugh paused to sigh and lowered his voice. "However, in this case, if you all agree to allow your children to attend three years at Mera Academy with a full academic scholarship, we will waive the lawsuit."

The parents looked at one another, then around the room at the Council members. The news of their children breaking laws was shocking enough, but Hugh's proposal was even more surprising. Mera Academy was a highly sought-out educational institution known to produce global leaders. It seemed inconceivable to reward the children with the finest educational resources available in the world for a grievance, especially one like this. They wondered why the Council had chosen their children, and if there was something it wasn't disclosing.

CHAPTER TWELVE

THE VASE AT GROMMEL LAKE

The next day, the rest of the Grommel battalion returned home, accompanied by the humans, the King, and several Clades. The vase at the end of the lake turned slowly and gracefully. It had never been used to transport humans before. Even Clades were usually prohibited from traveling to Earth, because their powers could be exposed to the humans. For this special mission, like the one to save the Regal Deer, Clades would risk the journey to return the children home safely.

Grommels were gathering near the vase to watch the aerial bridges that would open soon. While the children were saying their goodbyes, Grommel porters examined the vase to find the bridge that led closest to the Hoise Farm in Barrenville. Porters also assisted travelers' transitions into the torrent that directed them onto the right aerial bridge.

"It is time," a porter said. Four Loomers, led by Al'Visca, walked through the crowd of Grommels. Each Loomer approached a human with whom he could be aligned, as the Loomers' powers made them the Clade best suited to guide the humans home safely. Once all four had a match, they stood in rows of two facing the vase.

"Once they are in the Stewards' care, you must return immediately or risk exposing your powers to the humans," the King told the Loomers.

"Of course," the four Loomers nodded.

The first Loomer grasped Jill's arms, and together they walked toward the vase and entered the torrent. As they approached, the vase's gravitational pull intensified, until it drew them into its atmosphere. The waters immediately surrounding the vase converted into a fine mist, and an aerial bridge appeared, protruding from the vase. During the torrent, the vase's structure appeared hazy and smudged, nearly impossible to distinguish. The other three children waiting in line were amazed. After observing how Jill and the Loomer traveled, they were less frightened, but still nervous. Marilyn and her Loomer, then Ray and his, followed in sequence. Before Marilyn disappeared into the vase, she turned back to look at her brother and to glance one last time at her Norefolian friends. The King next approached Peet.

"Do I really have an ancestral power?" Peet asked.

"A power will reveal itself at its own time," the King said with a smile.

"Why couldn't I find it here?" Peet asked.

"This is a land where ancient powers thrive," the King said. "Perhaps the chisel you always carried prevented you from discovering it here."

"The chisel?" Peet asked. "I haven't known what to do with it, other than use it as a weapon against Cone Witches."

"The chisel is more than a keepsake or a weapon. It is a remnant of the Regal Deer and all of its unprecedented powers. The Regal Deer was unique among all the other creatures on Earth, because it was the most effective natural guardian of the grassland biome and helped maintain a balance among all life communities. The line of the Regal Deer's ancestors extends as far back as the creation of Norefole, as far back as my own ancestors' line. Someday, by your very hand, the chisel will repair the tear in the heart valve of the grasslands, and perhaps even release the Regal Deer from its tomb before it's too late."

Peet now believed he was destined for greatness and possessed some awesome power. The King observed, amused, how Peet stood taller, with his hands on his hips and a glimmer in his eyes. "You must safeguard your sister and Jill," the King said, putting his hand on Peet's shoulder. "I just had a terrible vision—the Elicitors were roaming around Barrenville. You know they are aware of Marilyn's powers. And Mangar appeared to have a curiosity about Jill, so the Elicitors might try to locate them. You

120

must shield and protect them from those who may want to exploit them, as the Elicitors have done with the four Clades."

"You must leave now, before the side of the vase turns away and the image disappears," Al'Visca said.

The Loomer, Al'Urg, whispered to Peet. "I promise you this will be far more of an adventure than the capillary you came through." The King nodded to Al'Urg, who clenched Peet's forearm and walked toward the vase. Just before Peet could respond, he felt the gravitational pull and saw the Loomer's image transform into an energetic force, though it maintained a recognizable shape. Peet felt dampness as they traversed the aerial bridge, cloaked in a thick fog of mist. Peet secured the chisel in his pocket. Then, he turned his head back and waved goodbye.

The Loomer and Peet became weightless as the air became lighter. Now fully on the aerial bridge, Peet again looked behind him, but could see only fog. He felt his feet touching the bridge and moving across it. Occasionally, he would grip the wooden rails. The travel home had no throttle, struggle, or push. The fog finally cleared, and Peet's eyes grew wide in wonder as he saw patches of farmland, woods, and the great lake. The aerial bridge somehow extended all the way to his hometown. As they neared Barrenville, Peet could make out Settlers' Hills in the distance, with its massive series of domes. They stepped off the aerial bridge and onto the soil of Hoise Farm.

Ray, Jill, and Marilyn were already on the ground when Peet and Al'Urg descended. "No peanuts, but that was the best flight ever!" Ray stated.

"We went through a flock of birds over the lake," Marilyn said, giggling.

"It's good to be on home soil again, isn't it, Peet?" Jill asked, as she patted him on the back.

The four Loomers led the children to Mera Lab. Once inside, they were greeted by the receptionist, who was also a Clamper. "Welcome, Loomers. How was your trip?" she asked the Clades.

"Traveling with Marilyn was like carrying a clumsy sheep through a land of wolves," the eldest Loomer responded. Marilyn sneered at the Loomer, and they all chuckled.

While in the elevator, the eldest Loomer quickly reminded them to keep all of Norefole secret. Wanerhess was going to handle explaining the children's whereabouts to their parents.

"He's right," Ray said, looking at Marilyn, Jill, and Peet. "Who would believe us anyway?"

The conference room was completely surrounded by glass walls, and jutted slightly out over the farmland. The parents watched their children pass through the glass corridor, followed by four tall strangers. As the weary children clumped together at the doorway, they appeared somehow aged in their demeanor and somewhat timid in their disposition, but healthy overall. The parents immediately ran over to them, relieved they were safe.

Although only one night had passed on Earth, the children had spent several days in the timeless world of Norefole. Wanerhess gave the parents and children a few moments to reunite while the Loomers visited with their fellow Norefolians, the Stewards who made up the Council. Shortly thereafter, the receptionist walked into the room with an exquisite tray of ripe Norefolian and local fruits. "We have been developing a new genus of fruit here at the lab," Wanerhess said, to prevent any unwanted questions.

Wanerhess, who sat at the farthest end of the table, then reined in the multiple conversations and called the room to order. All took a seat and focused their attention on him. "First, thank you to our visiting alumni for guiding the children back to us safely," he began, while looking at the four Loomers. "We discovered the disturbance in the grassland root system when the moon's rays highlighted it within our town. When we went to investigate it, we found a trail of four sleeping bags leading from the tent to the puncture, so we knew where to focus our search. Parents, while you slept, we tracked the children's footsteps away from the Sepvan house in the direction of Settlers' Hills.

"The children were found sleeping in one of our barns overnight," Wanerhess winked at the children. The parents' faces again expressed sheer shock.

"Ray!" his father exclaimed.

"Now, before you scold him," Wanerhess continued, "you must also know they performed a much greater good that outweighs any violations of our town's laws. Hence our proposal to you earlier."

"You see, while combing the ground for water veins, we discovered a rare, invasive species of cone seedling that had started to take root here in Settlers' Hills," one Council member said. "If allowed to spread further, it would have caused far more damage than the small tear in the root metropolis from the pond."

"In time, the cone seedling could have destroyed all we have accomplished and killed the native grasslands," another Council member said. "Your children unintentionally alerted us to this danger. Barrenville owes them for this, however it came to be."

"If you are in agreement with our proposal, each child will receive a full scholarship to Mera Academy, as well as a stipend for mandatory annual travel." The children smiled from ear to ear. Knowing that the Council members were actually Norefolian Stewards, they had an idea of just how far that travel might take them.

Ansel listened very carefully to Wanerhess and the Council. Although he respected them all greatly, he could not overcome a feeling of skepticism. He felt there had to be a better reason for their generosity, beyond mere gratitude. Just then, the youngest Loomer reached across the table for a pod of fruit. The parents watched as he easily split open the hard pod shell and plucked out its seeds.

Observing Ansel's skepticism and uneasiness, another Council member chimed in. "They are, after all, responsible for saving this quarter's production of hybrids. As you know, our hybrids are what finance the preservation of Barrenville's native root system. There is no price for this."

Jill reached for a banana and ate it, while Ray helped himself to an apple. Marilyn nearly crawled across the table to grab a pod, but was startled when Hady told her not to touch it.

"Why, Mom?" she asked.

"Because you might have an allergic reaction to it," Hady responded shyly. "I don't know what that is exactly."

"But, I've had them before at Cradle..." Marilyn began. She realized her mistake when Peet hit her under the table.

"Where?" Hady asked.

"Here, Mom, at the farm," Marilyn responded.

Hugh nodded to Al'Urg, which prompted him to ask, "If you don't need anything further, we must be leaving now."

"Thank you for everything," Hady said, noticing odd spots under the stranger's chin as he got up to leave.

"Of course, Madam," Al'Urg replied. The four strangers who accompanied the children to Barrenville then immediately returned home.

After a long discussion about the details of the children's future education, the meeting concluded in the late hours. The parents and children traveled down the elevator together. When they reached the driveway and turned back to face Mera Lab, they could see the Council members scattered throughout the glass room. Whatever they were discussing, Ansel had a hunch there was still more to the story than what the Council revealed to them. The weary children went to their respective cars, while the parents remained alongside the driveway.

"This is a once-in-a-lifetime opportunity," Ray's father said proudly. "We would be letting our children down if we didn't give them permission to attend Mera Academy. The condition is that all of us have to agree to this. It's an opportunity not even money can buy. Plus, the last thing I want is a lawsuit."

Jill's mother agreed. "If they are admitted together, they'll also continue to grow up together," she added.

Hady agreed as well, but worried about Marilyn, who was six years younger than the others. It was obvious that Ansel stood alone in his suspicions, and was outnumbered five to one. Nonetheless, Peet and Marilyn were his children. He would decide this matter privately with the family before deciding whether Peet and Marilyn should attend Mera Academy.

When the Sepvans arrived home, Peet went straight to his room. As he lay down on his bed, the chisel in his pocket brushed up against his hip. He placed it on his chest, which bumped his pendant. He gripped both, and a floodgate of questions opened. "What is this power the King spoke of? Have I always carried it? I wonder if my great, great, great grandparents knew of such powers. Why should humans be different from Clades anyway?" He soon fell into a deep slumber.

CHAPTER THIRTEEN

THE SEPVAN HOME

Mera Academy was located inside Settlers' Hills, tucked between Mera Lab to the south and the crop-production domes to the east. The school had a single floor of moderately sized classrooms for all the pre-college classes, and an above-ground, oversized basement that housed the library, cafeteria, and a small theater. The school also had a separate facility for recreational purposes, which doubled as a donation center on weekends. Immediately west of the complex was an extensive field of grasses, which contained part of the prairie path that proceeded to a forest. Just north of the school, two rows of three enormous and aged, blue-spruce pines formed a rainbow pattern. To the students, the space between the rows became known as Six-Pine Alley. As no other pines existed near the school, some children used the space between them as a corridor of sorts, or as a hiding place.

On Peet and Marilyn's first day, Hady drove them to the Academy and walked with them into the school. The principal greeted them in the lobby, as did their teachers. "Welcome to Mera Academy!" Principal Zenbar said. "This must be Peet and Marilyn." The children nodded. "We've been waiting for you. I am Principal Zenbar and I'm delighted to meet you." Two women joined them in the lobby. "Ms. Scalzo here will be Peet's instructor, and Ms. Smith will be Marilyn's," the principal said as she pointed to each of the instructors.

The lobby of the school formed a perfect, narrow rectangle. The administrative offices were to the left of the main entrance door and the classrooms to the right. Immediately opposite the main entrance was a long, glass music room with wooden and brass instruments left outside its door.

Hady noticed that the children passing through the lobby were well composed and orderly, unlike those at her children's previous school. As Marilyn and Peet were hastily escorted away by their new instructors, Hady knew her children were on a new path in life. The transition went much smoother than expected, she thought. "Funny, I don't hear any of the children," she said to the principal. "Why is it so quiet here?"

"Ah yes, today we observe silent day, where we practice solitude, inner reflection, focus, and meditation," Principal

Zenbar said. "The children must maintain strict silence while in school, and can express themselves only through written communication on notation devices distributed this morning. Instructors do not lecture today, but rather provide assignments. During each class period, students read material according to subject matter. Recess will also be a quiet period, but we'll have sensory activities."

"And tomorrow?" Hady asked worriedly.

"Tomorrow is a regular day. We begin each morning by having the children file into lines and face the flag in the lobby at exactly eight-thirty. The children rotate classes as the day progresses. We find it important to change their environment throughout the day as they change subject matter. Each themed classroom, after all, is conducive to a specific subject. Friday mornings are usually the children's favorites because we invite special guests to our library for storytelling followed by a two-hour period of library exploration. We also have special programs, which are listed in our comprehensive school calendar. It is included in these take-home packets, along with a school-supply list," Principal Zenbar said as she handed Hady the packets, one for each child.

"Thank you," Hady said, noticing the thickness of the two packets.

"I'm always accessible if you need to reach me. My contact information is on the inside of those packets."

"I appreciate that. Good day, Ms. Zenbar," Hady replied as she headed out the door.

Hady spotted Wanerhess walking up the school's front stairway with his hands tucked deep in the pockets of his overalls.

"Wanerhess!" Hady exclaimed, glad to see an old family friend at her children's new school.

"Mrs. Sepvan, your children will be fine here," he said, noting her worry. "They'll be well taken care of. I hope you realize how lucky they are to have been accepted here."

"So I keep hearing, but it is their first day at a new school, and I can't help but feel they will be lost for a while," she responded.

"Nonsense. They won't have time for themselves. There's much to explore here and many people to meet."

"Well, I'd best be on my way," Hady said. "I have new uniforms to tailor and school supplies to buy."

"Of course. Have a good day, Mrs. Sepvan." Wanerhess entered the school and Hady continued toward the parking lot.

Later that afternoon, the children returned home on the Mera Academy shuttle bus. Upon entering the house, they were struck by the aroma of their mother's homemade lasagna. Hady had prepared a special dinner for them in honor of their first day at the Academy. As was routine, the children set their bags and shoes against the coat closest at the entrance and headed into the kitchen to greet their mother. Peet and Marilyn sat on the stools at the kitchen counter, admiring the lasagna still crisping in the glass cookware nestled on old-world-themed linen.

"Did you recognize anyone at the Academy from around town?" Hady asked. The children shook their heads.

"I picked up most of the school supplies on the list, and I plan to get the rest tomorrow. Did you need any of it on your first day?"

"No, Mom," Peet responded. "We'll be okay without supplies for our first week."

"Good, now go and get cleaned up for dinner," Hady said. "Your father should be home soon."

When they returned to the kitchen, Peet and Marilyn sat together at the rectangular kitchen table on the L-shaped bench. Hady served each of them a brick-sized, cheese-smothered slice of lasagna. Peet ate three pieces, each smaller than the last, while Marilyn just had a single serving.

"Tell me, how was your first day?" Hady asked.

"Mom, the classrooms are nothing like Fareens," Marilyn said. "They have teacher aides for every kid, and all us kids have white pet tadpoles. For recess, we played inside a gigantic, decorated teepee with danglers hanging from it."

"Teepee danglers? Well, new school, new vocabulary," Hady said.

After dinner, Hady instructed Marilyn to try on the new uniform she had begun tailoring, in case any alternations were needed.

When Marilyn and Hady left the kitchen, Peet decided to organize his eco-jars on the wire shelf along the patio. As he held one of his many eco-jars, he reminisced about all the different terrains he had visited recently—the blue-speckled white sands near the Whimsical Tree, the dirt from Vesumio, the sand from

Cradle Desert, a limestone rock from Grommel Lake, and the Kingdom's rich soil. "I should have carried a bunch of plastic sandwich bags to fill with specimens from each of those places," Peet whispered to himself. "I could have added Norefole eco-jars to my collection."

Peet walked into the yard and toward the pond. There were still exposed roots, braided within the clear, gutted circle. He lay down on the grass next to the pond, and gripped the chisel he always kept with him. He lay facing the sky, brushing his hand over the roots, reflecting on the day all of them followed Gromyko into the capillary. A light, calming breeze moved in as he watched the clouds passing over Barrenville. Since the discovery of the capillary, he knew life would never be the same again for his sister, his two friends, or himself. Their experiences in Norefole had expanded their own world forever, and he felt extraordinarily lucky for that. "We are very sorry for harming you," he said aloud to the grasses. "We will not disturb you ever again."

A few moments later, Ansel stood over Peet. "I'd like to believe you and your sister have gained a new respect for these grasses and learned why we have certain rules in place."

"Yes, Dad," Peet responded.

"Come on, get off the grasses and let's go inside." Peet got up and walked inside the house to watch television with his father.

At Mera Academy, education focused principally on communication. They learned multiple languages—including Latin and an ancient language called Narfiel—and mathematics and science, which were treated like mandatory secondary languages. Children were also trained in techniques for attracting, stabilizing, and diffusing energy, centering their focus, and neutralizing feelings and emotions. It was an art form designed to harvest the reservoir of energies within the self.

Unlike Peet, Jill, and Ray—whose curriculum involved more lecture—Marilyn attended lab sessions. During a session, Marilyn and several other students entered the recreational center's basement, which was partitioned into six empty, large rooms. The recreation center was designed so that students could practice developing their skills under the direct supervision and guidance of a Steward. The head Steward in charge of the Academy, Hugh, knew every student by name, family, power, skill level, and interests. Class designation was not determined by age, but rather by factors like mental and emotional intelligence and energy skill level.

Peet had been so busy with the Academy and its heavy curriculum that he had not had time to visit the Whimsical Tree and the Genets a second time. During recess, Peet approached Hugh, who had befriended him, and inquired about the Whimsical Tree near the lake.

"The three Genets told me that I would be part of the Regal Deer's legacy, and I know the Regal Deer is the grassland's key species," Peet said solemnly. "The King himself said I would someday help protect the grassland biome, but I have not discovered the truth in any of this."

"We are already seeing your possibilities, Peet," Hugh

responded. "Not only are avalanches noticeable, but so are the slight ripples in the waters caused by the winds or by a butterfly's flutter a thousand miles away. These events have impact as well." Peet looked at him, rather confused. "You have already affected the root metropolis, and time will reveal it. Have you come into contact with it since your return?" Hugh asked.

"No," Peet replied.

"Are you sure?" Hugh asked again, causing Peet to think he must be mistaken. Peet thought for a while.

"Well, I patted the exposed roots in our backyard and apologized for disrupting them, but how would you know?" Peet asked.

The recess bell rang, a signal to return to class. "The root metropolis is very alive, Peet," Hugh said. "And it listens."

During the next several class periods, Peet tried to make sense of Hugh's comments. He yearned to get home and check on the pond again. The last hour of class felt four times that long.

Upon returning home, Peet darted to the backyard to search for the pond, but could not find it. He bent down on his hands and knees and crawled around the shrubs, looking for where the pond had been. All traces of it had disappeared. He ran into the house to get Marilyn. She was already in her room, repositioning her dolls along the perimeter of her bedroom.

"Marilyn, did you do anything to make the pond disappear?" he asked.

"What? No! It's gone? Let me go see," she said. They both ran to the backyard. "How did it disappear?"

"I'm not sure, but the native grasses couldn't have grown over the hole that quickly since yesterday," Peet said. They both stood there, transfixed, on the spot where the pond had been.

Marilyn placed both her index finger and middle finger in the center of her forehead and closed her eyes. She tracked her fingers down to the center of her nose, back and forth.

"Marilyn? Are you okay?" Peet asked, but she ignored him.

She was very intense and looked like she was going to sneeze, but never did. She opened her eyes and, with both of her hands, began to quickly pluck at the air, screaming, "Catch the wisps! Catch the wisps, Peet!" Peet saw nothing other than his sister jumping around, looking like she was trying to poke soap bubbles in the air.

"Marilyn?" Peet said.

"They're floating all around us, Peet. Catch them."

"Okay, what do they look like, so I can help?" he asked, thinking she had gone mad.

"Open your eyes, Peet. Can't you see them? They are tiny wisps!" Marilyn was bouncing around the grass, reaching out in all directions, collecting the wisps, then patting herself and Peet.

"What are you doing?" Peet asked.

"Don't you see the gush of wisps from where the pond used to be? They are small bundles of energy. My Steward said that disrupted areas of the biome will always expel a surge of wisps once they've finished healing themselves. She said we should collect these gifts from nature so they can cling to us and become part of our own energy fields. Come on, Peet. Catch them!"

Peet was astonished by Marilyn's mature understanding of the inner workings of the biome. As he watched her hopping on and near the former pond, he became confused and disappointed as to why he could not see the wisps. He watched her do this exercise until she exhausted herself.

"Come on, Sis, enough physical activity for one afternoon. Let's go inside and have a snack." He put his arm around her and walked her back into the house toward the kitchen. While Peet towered over Marilyn, both of them always managed to simultaneously plunge their faces into the refrigerator when looking for their preferred snacks.

Peet decided not to ask her any more about the wisps. Nevertheless, along with her bursts of power in Norefole, this was the second time he felt he could learn from his younger sister.

*　　*　　*

The next day, Saturday morning, Peet awoke to the sound of birds enveloping the house with their chirping songs. It sounded as if the birds were equipped with perches and microphones alongside the perimeter of the house. He peered out his bedroom window while extending his arms over his head to stretch. Birds were all over the trees and shrubs in front of the house. He could count hundreds, perhaps even thousands of birds. He instinctively went to the chest and placed the chisel in his pajama pocket. He popped into Marilyn's room to tell her about the birds, but she was gone. He heard the voices of his parents and sister in the family room, discussing the unusual volume of birds swarming around the house.

"Good morning, darling," Hady said.

"Good morning," Peet responded. "Where did all these birds come from?"

"We don't know," Ansel replied. "In all the years we've lived here, we've never seen anything like it."

Marilyn pressed her body against the patio screen, curious about the sheer number of birds. "Why aren't the birds scattered around any of the other houses?" she asked.

"Perhaps these birds are from a single flock and wisely chose our house as a rest stop," Ansel said. He chuckled with worry. Peet had a hunch that the birds were there because of either his sister or himself—and possibly both—yet he didn't know their purpose.

Peet walked to the patio door behind Marilyn. One of the birds flew down to the patio and hopped over to the screen door. Peet realized that the bird was examining them, not just looking for food scraps. Peet was frozen at the patio door, until Marilyn yelled out, "They're going to come into the house!" The bird spread its wings, tilted its head back, and let out an ominous screech. All the birds took flight at once, with the bird from the patio leading the way.

"Well, it looks like they're moving on to their next pit stop," an anxious Ansel commented. Peet watched the birds fly east toward the lake in one large flock, and felt compelled to head in the same direction.

Because the birds woke them up just after sunrise, the Sepvans ate an early breakfast, then each one went about their errands for the day. Peet decided that if he left soon, he would have enough time to visit with the Genets and be home well before dinner. He put on his hiking shoes and grabbed a jacket on his way out. The sky soon turned silver, and it began to drizzle. Feeling good that he had time to spare outdoors, and with his rain jacket on, he skipped part of the way down the path.

He reached the section of the path where he had exited when he discovered the Whimsical Tree, so he veered off the path. As he traveled northeast, the land became more difficult to hike. The forest was denser and the branches more tangled than before. "This might not be the same way I went last time," Peet thought to himself. A short while later, he stumbled across old, rusty train tracks that seemed out of place. He recalled his grandfather had once told him about a railroad track running close to the lake. His grandfather said goods used to be shipped between neighboring territories separated by the lake. Cargo arriving in Barrenville was loaded onto the railway and transported to a train depot in the next town. Other trains would then distribute the goods to cities across the country.

"This must be a splinter of tracks from the prairie path that leads to the lake. Perfect!" Peet whispered as he followed it. The barely visible track was well covered with underbrush, as it had been abandoned for decades. "I should have come to it by now." Peet stopped to lift and rotate his head, having been hunched over to follow the tracks. To his right, he spotted a small woodshed in the distance. The light around the shed was darker than anywhere else nearby, like looking out at the ocean and notices the deeper waters appear to be darker blue. Peet got the idea to use the abandoned shed as a private clubhouse. As he walked toward it, the temperature dropped. It felt somehow familiar. He stopped to look behind him and listened. All was still and quiet, so he pressed onward.

After a few more steps, Peet heard a loud ruckus in the opposite direction. It sounded like the swarm of birds he had heard earlier that morning. He turned in the direction of the noise and walked toward it, veering well away from the shed. Almost immediately, the sunlight pierced the silver-veiled sky, the air was warmer, and his surroundings became somehow more peaceful. He ran, now more energized, jumping over fallen branches, bubbling streams, and a few granite boulders, until he arrived at the unusually tall, intertwined trees that separated the rest of the woods from the clearing that led to the lake and the Whimsical Tree. The birds, perched on and around the intertwined trees, drew silent as Peet approached. He passed cautiously through the unusual alignment of trees. The clearing was just as scenic and fragrant as he remembered. An overly exuberant Peet burst into a run, all the way until he reached the dome of branches from the Whimsical Tree peering just beyond the cliff. He couldn't wait another moment to share his adventures in Norefole with the Genets.

As he approached the cliff, Peet saw that the waves immediately below, with their scaled silver interiors, appeared to be constantly drifting rather than rolling back and forth as they had done before. Some of the Whimsical Tree's exposed roots appeared disjointed; someone or something had tampered with them. Even some of the roots along the cliff were now dangling, partly detached from the tree trunk.

Peet arrived at the doorway of the tree and noticed the "Genets" sign had fallen to the ground. He felt the cool mist of the lake waters brush against his back. When Peet knocked on the door, it opened, and he entered slowly. The chandelier had shattered on the floor, and the white interior of the tree as well as the white furniture had been charred. The signs on the various doors were missing or had fallen off, and most of the door latches were broken. Peet called out for the Genets, but no one responded. Their home, the Regal Deer itself, had been broken into, vandalized, and left abandoned.

"How long have the Genets been missing?" Peet wondered. "Could they have returned to Norefole? No, they wouldn't have abandoned the Regal Deer voluntarily, not even for a second." Then it hit him. "Is it really possible the Elicitors or the Cone Witch came to Barrenville and did away with the Genets?" Peet recalled what the King had told him of his vision of the Elicitors roaming Barrenville. As he explored around the inside of the tree, it shifted and inched downward toward the lake. Its roots were struggling to hold it to the edge of the cliff. Peet cautiously walked back through the parlor and toward the entrance door, when he saw the shadow of a bird.

Peet stopped, startled to see a bird perched on the mantel of the charred, white-brick fireplace. He wondered if it had flown in behind him, or perhaps it had come in through the fireplace. The bird sat perfectly still, examining Peet. In turn, Peet studied the bird, which was compact, stocky, and unusually large for a blackbird. It held a shell in its large beak. The bird leaned forward from the mantel and dropped a clam onto the wooden table below. The clam hit hard against the table, then fell to the ground, but did not open.

The bird squawked. It looked at Peet and then at the clam, as if directing him to tend to it. Peet knelt down to pick it up. He noticed that the clam had a small hole on one side. The hole was too small for his index finger, but perhaps it was big enough for the bird's beak to fit. The clam's shell was covered with countless embedded rings, and felt cold to the touch. Peet looked inside his pocket for an instrument small enough to fit the hole. The bird watched as Peet patted himself down. "Ah, the chisel should fit," he said, as he found the chisel in his pocket. He removed it, and gently inserted it into the hole in the clam.

The bird squawked a second time, but this squawk lingered longer and sounded louder. It made Peet uneasy, so he hesitated to open it. As he looked around the broken parlor, the destruction saddened him, and he felt a resurgence of purpose. He took the chisel point and inserted it perfectly into the clam. Immediately, the rings of the clam began to merge together into a thick, solid, black line in the center. The solid line then moved up, transferred onto the chisel, and spread across it before disappearing.

Without any further manipulation by Peet, the clam opened. The inside of the clam shell was colored shiny silver, and it had a pillowy mass that waddled greatly. "I haven't felt this good in hundreds of years!" the clam spoke. Surprised, Peet dropped the clam, which landed on his foot. "Ouch!" it said. Peet carefully picked up the clam, set it on the table, and sat on a chair nearby.

"Who, or what, are you?" Peet asked.

"I am a pulse in the waters who awakens every morning to a potent, warm sun and sleeps soundly to the rhythm of the night moon's pull on these waters," the clam said.

"How did your lines disappear?" Peet asked.

"The rings of time covered my body. You removed them, Peet. The rings represented my age, and now that you have taken away the rings, I am youthful again. Thank you." The clam now jiggled forcefully inside its shell to demonstrate its vitality and strength. The bird's head bobbed and followed the movement of the clam flopping in its shell. "Tonight, the waters below shall echo with the sound that you have returned to us."

"How do you know my name? And more importantly, do you know where the Genets have gone? What happened here?" Peet asked.

The clam stopped moving and distressfully stated, "The Cone Witch has returned to Barrenville. She transformed our beloved Genets into barren trees, but not before her Elicitors drew out their powers as they tried to defend the Regal Deer.

"The Norefolian King has the power to orchestrate entire communities to work together—the flocks in the air, creatures of

142

the land, and schools in the sea. He instructed certain wildlife of this area to safeguard the tree until your arrival. Therefore, the question is, how may we help you, Peet?" the clam asked. The bird squawked three times, while bobbing its head up and down.

The clam's words weighed heavily on Peet. "I don't understand," he said, frustrated. "I have no powers that can protect the tree, or get elicited, for that matter." He propped his feet up on his chair and placed the palm of his hand on his cheek while resting his elbow on his knee. The bird squawked again and flew down to the table's edge, across from Peet.

"Together, we might stand a chance to preserve the grassland biome and defeat the Cone Witch," the clam said. "But if we don't work together, this biome will be altered forever. It might not survive. We've already noticed that the land has destabilized, because there is a stronger undercurrent in the waters beneath the ground. Our time is critical now, so I must return to my clam fleet alongside this cliff. But first we must encourage the tree's roots to continue holding themselves to the side of the cliff." The bird squawked one last time before it swooped down to collect the clam, which was just then closing its shell. It took flight out the front door, dropping the clam near the edge of the plateau. Peet followed behind, waving his arms and signaling for the bird to return, but it did not.

"So the Witch survived and has returned to Barrenville, and with Elicitors, too," Peet said to himself. "How could they have gotten past the Grommels?"

As he pondered these questions, someone approached him

slowly from behind. Peet felt the sand swoosh near him, causing him to turn his head. Just then, an Elicitor shoved him off the plateau and into the cold waters below.

"What did you do that for?" another Elicitor asked. "He had a very distinct energy. Didn't you feel an unusual energy about him?"

"He was trespassing on our Ascentia," replied the Elicitor who pushed Peet. "The energy is coming from the Ascentia. Haven't you had Genet powers before? Don't you see the tree's roots extend below, alongside the cliff? The human was standing right next to them." Both Elicitors observed the water for a while, and turned away once satisfied that Peet did not return to the surface.

"When we arrived in Barrenville, the Witch had us squelch the powers from those three Genets. Then she had us drag them into the woods so she could transform them more easily. Now, she has us working on the Ascentia. Not much has changed for us from one world to the next," the Elicitor said to the other.

"You forget the rarity of this Ascentia, which will redefine our kind. Come, we have a lot more antlers to pull off its body," the other said as he ripped out another large root. "Eliciting is a lot easier than this kind of manual labor."

"Let's get back to the top and get more help. There is too much left."

Peet heard his own voice leave his body as he drew closer to the water. In a glimpse of a moment, he envisioned the faces of his family and friends, the Barrenville landscape, and his memories of Norefole. Then came the sharp pain of entering the waters, which enveloped him. Without putting up a fight, he became an anchor, destined to move swiftly downward and rest on the bottom of the lake. As he was settling on the idea of never returning, a fleet of clams surrounded him, clenching his clothes from every direction. Upon sensing the many little creatures attempting to rescue him, Peet shook off his resignation. "I survived the plunge," he thought. He realized he could not stall any longer, and became determined to swim to the surface at any cost. The water's hold began to feel like an enemy, as its icy clutches compressed him from every direction. He was in tremendous pain. As he reached the surface, he desired nothing more than to exit the malicious waters.

The clams tugged his waterlogged body to the side of the cliff against some roots, where the Elicitors could not see him. Knowing that Elicitors had pushed him and would be watching the waters, Peet coughed into his elbow to muffle any sound he might produce. Peet shivered violently as he waited in the cold waters for the Elicitors to leave. He hugged a large root with his trembling body, like holding onto an elephant's trunk. Gradually, the temperature of the root intensified, which produced a comforting heat that warmed Peet's body and relieved his pain. The Elicitors' voices finally deadened, and Peet felt safe to climb back up. He patted the root and thanked the Regal Deer for helping him. Although cut and bruised, Peet now had the strength to hoist himself back up the cliff.

He carefully approached the rim of the plateau, with his

chisel in hand like a weapon. The door of the tree was wide open. He saw no movement inside except for a light he had not seen before, which cascaded through the parlor. Peet looked up at the cloudless sky. There was no apparent reason for the strange light, not even the sun reflecting on a shiny surface of something in the parlor. Once on the plateau, Peet stood to the side of the doorway, listening for movement or voices, but heard none. Searching for the source of this strange light, Peet climbed the branches of the Whimsical Tree, up to the cliff above. When he reached the top of the cliff's edge, his eyes opened wide as he again saw the cascading light, now rippling over the clearing, all the way from the spot where he stood.

He stood tall at the rim of the cliff, catching his breath from the climb while holding the chisel by his side. He sensed intense heat emanating from it. He gripped it tighter and found it felt lighter, as if the marrow had been hollowed out. As Peet scrutinized the chisel, its rugged outer layer slowly flaked off, revealing part of an antler. Once the bark coat had been shed completely, the smooth antler expelled an energetic shock that pierced into Peet's palm, and then traveled up his arm. He dropped the chisel on the ground. When he looked at the top of his hands, wrists, and inner arms, Peet noticed his skin had a very faint, red, web-like appearance. Peet pulled up his shirt to check his abdomen and chest, and he also checked his legs, but found no markings there. He wondered if the effects had also transferred to his face. He thought he would have a hard time explaining such markings to his parents. When he picked up the chisel, he was neither scared of it nor bewildered by its effects, but he knew he had to get home before it got any later.

Peet once again found himself at the porch stairs, with little memory of his trek home through the woods or his travels on the prairie path. He went straight to the bathroom and removed his shirt, pants, and socks. Nervously, he looked in the mirror. He did not find any more of the faint, web-like pattern on his body, but he did discover bruises from the impact of hitting the waters. He jumped in the shower and scrubbed his hands and arms, but the web pattern would not fade, despite how hard he scrubbed. "Oh, no! How am I ever going to explain this?" Peet asked out loud. Peet then heard a loud knock on the door.

"Dinner's on," Ansel said.

"Okay, Dad, I'll be right out," Peet responded.

Peet wore long-sleeved, flannel pajamas to the table. Since starting at Mera Academy, Marilyn had stopped creating her cereal-box fortress, so there would be no sight barriers between her, Peet, and their parents. He worried about the markings on his hands, and hid them as often as he could. Hady had prepared a casserole, a family favorite. A famished Peet ate quickly, then excused himself to go to his room. He jumped into bed, and settled into the freshly washed bamboo sheets. Instead of doing homework, he reminisced about Norefole, and soon fell into a deep, heavy sleep.

In his dream, he stood in the middle of a sea of tall grasses, extending his arms into the grass and running through it as if he were a glider plane. Time and obligation became irrelevant. He approached some trees atop a distant hill. On the horizon, he saw the Kingdom. He stood still to take in the scenery and breathe the crisp, fresh air. He felt remarkably renewed and weightless, possessing an energy he had never felt in his entire life. He looked down at his exposed arms and hands, to see that the web-like pattern had disappeared. He searched his pants pocket for the chisel, but it was gone. He patted his other pocket, but no chisel there either. He realized it was back in his bedroom chest, and he knew he was far from home. Peet decided to linger longer in the wild grasses, eventually deciding that he would head toward the Kingdom for a visit. He relished his time in the grasses, performing acrobatics in all directions and gazing at the clouds.

Suddenly, Peet caught a glimpse of a familiar flash of emerald gems coming through the grasses. "You're in danger, Peet!" Gromyko yelled.

"Gromyko! I'm so happy to see you," Peet responded, not feeling any sense of foreboding or surprise.

"Now is not the time for playing or lounging," Gromyko said. "You must get back, Peet. Please!"

Peet looked at him more closely and saw the distraught look in his expression. "I think I am dreaming, Gromyko. How do I get back?" Peet asked.

"Well, can you scare yourself enough so that you might wake up?" Gromyko asked.

"How am I going to scare myself?" Peet asked.

"Peet! Peet! You slept in. You're going to miss the shuttle bus.

I thought you were ready by now," a worried Hady said, as she searched hastily through his closet for a clean uniform.

"Good call, Gromyko. Missing the shuttle would alarm anyone..." said Peet, still not fully awake.

"Who is Gromyko?" Hady asked. "It's a good thing your father dropped Marilyn off earlier. She's already had her recital practice." Peet sprang out of bed, realizing he was not dreaming anymore. As he scrambled to get ready for school, he wondered why he would be in danger.

Peet arrived at school during recess and immediately headed to Hugh's office to tell him about his encounters with the clam and the Elicitors. After meeting with Hugh, Peet found Jill on the playground and repeated the story he had told Hugh. Peet also told her about what happened to him at the Whimsical Tree with the chisel. "The web pattern is gone, so I didn't say anything to Hugh about that."

"I'm horrified," she said. "You could have drowned, Peet."

"Hugh is sending for Clampers to patrol these grounds as we speak. And remember, we can't tell Ray any of this. He doesn't even know about Marilyn's skills yet."

"Why do you suppose the King told us not to tell him?" Jill asked. "Don't you find that a bit strange?"

"I saw O'tis signal to the King right before he told us not to tell Ray. In fact, now that I think about it, you and I don't share most of our classes with Ray either," Peet said.

The school bell sounded, signaling the end of recess, so the children re-entered the school. Peet felt uneasy throughout the

149

rest of the day. He sensed something brewing in the distance.

CHAPTER FOURTEEN

ELICITORS ABOUND

Ray was an only child and usually played alone. One late afternoon near dusk, while he was kicking a soccer ball around, a stranger approached him. The stranger was elegant, having a tall and lean stature, as well as a commanding presence about him. He smiled at Ray.

"Norefole misses you," the charismatic stranger said.

"You are from Norefole?" Ray responded, observing the familiar double-tailed cloak used throughout the Kingdom.

"Yes. My name is Mangar."

"I am Ray. Has something happened back in Norefole that you have come all this way?"

"Yes, it's time you come join the best of us Clades. You know your powers, correct? Perhaps from the Steward training?"

"What Clade are you?"

"An Elicitor, of course."

"I've never met one of you before."

"Have you control of your powers yet?" Mangar asked, sensing a glimmer of Ray's powers awakening. "You don't remember why the Witch encapsulated you within a tree at Barren Woods, do you?" Ray shook his head. "I was there. The Witch tried to protect you from the other Clades and their King. They did not want you to learn the secrets of Norefole, as they did not trust you. Ray, you have important powers, and we need you to access them soon."

"How can I access a power I do not have, and why would my friends not trust me?" an intense Ray asked.

"Ah, a philosopher," Mangar said. "Typical Elicitor quality. What are those Stewards teaching you then, if not to access your power? Given your gifted nature, you should have realized your powers by now, like your youngest friend."

"You mean Marilyn? I don't know what you mean. Even if I had a power, why would I want to share it with a stranger? Aren't there Clades who could share their powers with you?" Ray recalled the celebratory dinner back in Norefole, where he listened to battle stories of how the other Clades had fought against the Elicitors and the Witch at the Five Clades Garden. If this was an Elicitor, Ray thought, they weren't anything to fear. "I have nothing to give to your Clade, or any Clade for that matter," an annoyed Ray said. He picked up his ball and started to walk back toward home. "I'd better get home before it gets any darker."

"When you discover your power, Ray, you will remember me," Mangar said. "I shall have something very special for you when that time comes."

Ray paused in his tracks. "How would you know what is special to me?" he demanded.

"I know more about you than you know of yourself. You'll see," Mangar responded. He turned to walk away, then vanished.

"You know nothing about me," a cocky Ray said out loud. Night came in a flash, as if a black-velvet curtain had dropped from the sky to darken the land and all that it contained.

*   *   *

Back at the palace in Norefole, the King met with the head Clades. "I can no longer sense the energies of our three Genets," he said. "I'm worried for them and the Regal Deer. It's time we engage the Grommels to return to Barrenville."

All the Clades agreed. Al'Visca's presence immediately became absent as he left his body behind, traveling out of the Kingdom and through the desert, brushing past Barren Woods until he arrived at Grommel Lake.

The King telepathically informed Gromyko that the Loomer would soon be approaching. Once the Grommel horn sounded, the troops gathered around the lake. Gromyko, with the Loomer now shadowing him, stood in the center of the lake, near the rotating vase, to address the other Grommels. "It's time we find those who've breached our aerial bridges and threatened Earth's root metropolis," Gromyko said. "Clades would only risk exposing their powers to humans. The Stewards have done all they can do to support and preserve the grassland biome. So it is now up to us to intervene before our enemies destroy it all. We match the Elicitors well in strength and tactics, especially on human soil."

"We are concerned that the Elicitors, with the possible help of a feeble Cone Witch, may have overpowered the Genets guarding the Regal Deer," Al'Visca said. "They would have elicited three Genet powers for a single use and exploited the Regal Deer. The Witch will also seek to plant her cone seedlings, to try to begin a new reign and replicate Barren Woods on Earth. If she succeeds, she will suffocate the dual-heart valve of the grassland biome. Both of our worlds are in grave danger, and we must stop them before it is too late."

"Who will join the troop for this mission?" Gromyko asked. As Al'Visca reluctantly returned to the Kingdom, leery of leaving the Grommels, he heard a unified, thundering Grommel roar echo throughout the fortress. He had learned that after the battle at the Five Clades Garden, their enemies had breached the aerial bridges and injured many Grommels.

Grog requested that those who wished go to Barrenville to hunt the Witch and her Elicitors remain after the horn sounded. As soon as it sounded again, all the female Grommels left the vicinity of the lake, along with the youngest and eldest. Unlike the males, female Grommels did not have the slivers on their lower backs to combat Elicitors. They were smaller than the males, but more agile. Rather than fight, they tended to their caverns, cared for their tadpoles, and—above all—protected the vase.

Grog observed that he could easily form a battalion from the Grommels who remained, but he could only send a dozen warriors. To determine who would go to Barrenville, Grog ordered the target game set up. The Grommels who remained moved to the same side of the lake. Grayle brought out a mesh ball, removed its covering, and threw it alongside the lake, opposite the others. The ball quickly expanded until it took the form of a sheet, covering the full length of the lake and nearly the height of the upper-floor caverns. The target sheet was made of finely textured mesh, making it lightweight and translucent, and wavered slightly in the wind. At its center was a narrow rectangle. The Grommels who remained each plucked a sliver from their lower back. Each of the slivers had a distinct scent, so it would be clear who came closest to their target.

Like the rest, Gromyko pulled a sliver from his lower back. At the sound of the horn, he and thirty-five others simultaneously leapt in the air and launched them. The slivers flew hard across the pond until they hit the sheet. After all thirty-six slivers had embedded their scents, Grayle approached the target from the upper caverns. Moving swiftly from left to right, she sniffed only within the rectangle, and announced which Grommels would to head to Barrenville the next day.

"You leave at dusk," Grog shouted. "Now go and be with your families." The mates of the chosen dozen immediately stepped forward to embrace them, for fear of their never returning. Gromyko was restless and desired to leave immediately, excited to get to Barrenville and finish his previous mission. He also sensed Peet needed him, but he would have to wait and leave with the others if they were going to succeed.

As was the tradition for Grommels sent into battle or on dangerous missions, the troops and their mates moved through the crowd for a full lap around the lake. The onlooking Grommels bowed as they passed, out of honor and respect. Aerial bridges were usually safe, but some Grommels, over time, had been lost—and this mission was extremely dangerous. The tadpoles of the chosen Grommels followed them from within the lake as they circled around it. One troop member, Greler, and his mate Grala—the youngest pair to have tadpoles—together reached into the lake until their young touched them. After their full lap, they too retired into their cavern. Grala held Greler close while they rested on their humble pad, and soon their tadpoles appeared in their small pool of water.

"You'll come back to us, won't you?" Grala asked.

"Although this is my first mission, I've been trained in the Grommel ways all my life," Greler said. "I'm also going with some of our best warriors. And don't forget, Gromyko is joining us, so our success is near certain." Grala nestled closer to him and fell asleep. When she awoke, Greler had gone.

An unexpected, light rainfall occurred early the next morning. The twelve Grommels gathered around the edge of the lake near the vase. They lined up in rows of two, with Gromyko and Greler first. A porter had found their destination on the vase and prepared the first pair for the torrent. The waters of the lake parted slightly, forming a path. When the torrent came, the two twirled into it gracefully.

All the Grommels watched as the two dispatched from the ground, following the torrent, and entered onto the aerial bridge. Only four glimmering specks of emerald eyes flashed when they faced the troop once more, then quickly disappeared. The rain suddenly got heavier and more concentrated in the vicinity of Grommel Lake. Six more Grommels made it into the vase. When the fifth pair of troops moved forward, the porters were already shaking their heads, preventing them from porting. The rain and heavy winds interfered with the torrent, which could potentially carry a Grommel to an unintended place, or worse, into a void. Only eight Grommels went to Barrenville on this mission.

*　　*　　*

Deep in the forest, the Cone Witch waited in a shed Mangar had built for her. The wound from Peet's chisel was toxic to her body, and with each passing day she grew weaker. She placed all her hope in her Elicitors—that they would succeed in combing the Regal Deer for a perfect specimen and extracting the Juso she so desperately sought. One afternoon, with the energy she had left, she began to puncture the nearby grounds in strategic places. Each time she punctured the ground, she plundered the native roots. She knew that puncturing the heart of the native grasses would not only weaken the root metropolis, but also prime the Barrenville land for the cone seedlings she kept within her own shell. Her three barren trees, made from the Genets, were a foreign species to Barrenville, and they too interfered with the native prairie root system.

In the meantime, the three Elicitors who had taken Genet powers were systematically tearing away the branches of the Whimsical Tree. With each new load of branches delivered to the Witch, less of the Regal Deer remained. Finally, leaving only a skeletal resemblance of a tree, the three Elicitors reported back to the Witch.

As the Witch punctured the grounds, the waters of Grommel Lake slowly filled with silt and other pollutants. The tadpoles congregated on the opposite side of the silt. The composition of the vase was in imminent danger, as multiple red threads now spun on the eternally rotating vase.

"Your Highness, although we have the Genet powers, we could not find energy to mine in that tree," one of the Elicitors said. "We tried to tell you before we dismembered it."

"I know the Juso exists in that Ascentia!" the Cone Witch yelled. "Must I do everything myself? Why couldn't you find a piece of the tree that carried some marrow before you tore it apart? You have Genet powers. Its energy should have been easy for you to find."

158

"We cannot elicit a power that does not exist," a second Elicitor replied.

"Are you trying to mine the energy for yourself?" she asked, scowling.

"No! Of course not, never. We would never turn from you," the Elicitor said nervously. "And it would only amplify our existing powers, rather than alter them like you could."

"The energy was there before, but when we returned to mine the tree, it no longer had an energy field," another Elicitor said. "No matter how much mass we took from it, we simply could not locate it. Not even in the stump." Neither the Elicitors nor the Witch could explain why the tree was lifeless, and therefore unresponsive to being elicited.

The Witch's eyes grew rounder, and the intensity in her face swelled. "You leaked out the power from the tree!" she screamed at the Elicitors. "How will I ever heal or have you retain any elicited power? How can I build a glorious Elicitor army with versatile powers if the marrow is gone? Who could have taken it? Did it leak into the lake? Is it on the ground near the cliff? You need to get Mangar and find out where that power went. Now!"

"We saw the same boy from the battle in Norefole at the tree and..."

"Silence!" she exclaimed, and then coughed. "Go find me this boy, and don't return without him." The Elicitors left and signaled to a fourth Elicitor, who had just arrived, to follow them to the spiral tree.

During his routine canvassing of the health of the native grasses, Wanerhess noticed something unusual about them. They appeared limp and less lustrous, and many had speckles along the blades. Wanerhess knew that if the native grasses were in this condition, the hybrids would be in worse shape. He took samples from throughout the fields for assessment at Mera Lab.

When he next tended to the hybrids, he noted they were tainted a soft-red hue, which he had never seen before. Wanerhess became gravely concerned. While he examined the root mesh atop one of the domes, emerald sparkles shimmered in the distance. The eight Grommels, in a single horizontal row, moved swiftly through the thicket of grasses and around the domes toward Wanerhess. "My dear friends," Wanerhess said. The Grommels collectively rumbled. "I suppose you are here to tell me why the grasses appear this way."

Gromyko pulled the grasses toward him to smell them. "These grasses have a faint cone smell I know too well," he said, starting to move away. "I'm afraid the Cone Witch has penetrated your root metropolis. To the Ascentia!" Gromyko exclaimed. Wanerhess watched as the eight Grommels moved swiftly east toward the lake. The Grommels believed their enemies would be exploiting the tree, and hoped to make a surprise attack by water.

*   *   *

The Elicitors revisited the tree and canvassed the whole area. One dove into the waters, then climbed up the cliff. He noticed ring-shaped, peeled areas on the cliff's sediment, and a similarly scraped tree root nearby. It looked as if someone or something had tried to climb up from the lake. Another Elicitor examined the blue-speckled sand on the tree's plateau for clues, while the third searched inside the tree's remaining stump and its few thick branches. Mangar appeared on the cliff above the plateau, where he found a few casings from what seemed to be bark scattered on the ground. He collected them and put them in his pocket.

As the Grommels reached the vicinity of the Whimsical Tree, they spotted the Elicitors. They approached slowly by water, and carefully climbed up to the first plateau. One Elicitor, the only one still holding Genet power, felt a familiar energy coming closer. From the plateau, he glanced down at the water and saw the contrast of the white bodies with emerald eyes alongside the cliff. "Grommels! Grommels!" he yelled. Mangar ordered the Elicitors to their defensive positions, while he ran back to the forest to protect the Witch.

With no time to waste, Mangar ripped the shed apart with his bare hands, turning it into mere panels scattered all around the Witch. He carried her to a cave deep into the forest. The Witch had left behind a torn-down shed, holes in the ground, three barren trees, and a dismembered tree as physical remnants of her presence. Once safely in the cave, Mangar laid her fragile body gently on the ground and waited with her the full night. They both knew that if the other Elicitors were destroyed, Mangar would be left to serve as the only conduit between the Witch and the powers they sought.

Meanwhile, some of the Grommel troops leaped onto the ledge of the plateau, and others leaped all the way up onto the higher cliff. In Norefole, the Grommels' slivers could interrupt the transference of powers and dissipate them. But on Earth, they served as small arrows, shooting with a raw velocity and power like that from a crossbow. The Elicitors had nowhere to run or hide, and had no Imaj or Loomer powers to use for escape. The Grommels prevailed in a short but decisive battle, destroying all three Elicitors without losing a single one of their own.

As they turned their attention to the tree stump, however, they were deeply saddened. The Regal Deer had passed. In the history of the Grommels, never before had they lost a key species of any biome. They were too late, and felt they had failed Norefole. Now they were more determined than ever to find the Cone Witch and any remaining Elicitors, and to save the Genets.

Back in Settlers' Hills, Wanerhess requested a special meeting of the Council. He reported that a small troop of Grommels had arrived in Settlers' Hills earlier in the day. "I'm afraid the Cone Witch has returned, and this time she brought Elicitors," Wanerhess said. "Gromyko confirmed the Witch's scent on the grasses, so she has interfered with our root system. The Grommels also informed me that the King fears the Genets are no longer guarding the Whimsical Tree. We all know the Genets would not have voluntarily left the Regal Deer unprotected. The Grommels are heading there now."

"Yes, Peet informed me earlier about an incident he had with a couple of Elicitors," Hugh said.

"They pushed him off a cliff into the lake. Peet was lucky to survive."

"There has also been a change in the appearance and texture of the grasses from the weakening of the root metropolis," Wanerhess said.

"The native grass roots are incredibly hardy and adaptable, especially in a mass concentration like the one we have here in Barrenville," another Council member said. "Her activities on this land may have changed the appearance of our grasses, but the only way the Witch could destroy the root metropolis is by planting the seeds of her own species in our fertile lands and then germinating them. Just a few cone tree roots placed in the right areas could be enough to collapse the dual-heart valve of the grassland biome."

"We must promptly learn the health of the Regal Deer," Wanerhess said. "It may be the only one that can repair such damage to the root metropolis."

"Speaking of the deer, where is Peet and this famous chisel of his now?" asked Reid, another Council member.

"Probably at home, since school is out," said a Council member named Ruth.

"Wanerhess, will you have Peet join us for the end of our meeting?" Hugh asked.

"Done!" Wanerhess said.

The Grommels continued their hunt through the forest in search of other Elicitors and the Cone Witch. Gromyko, however, headed to the Sepvans' home. Hady had been watering her small garden that afternoon when, out of the corner of her eye, she glimpsed at a couple of emerald jewels near the side of the house. She turned toward them, but they were gone. She passed the back of her hand against her face to move some hair that dangled in her eyes. Before she could turn the hose back on, she saw the emerald jewels flash again. "Hello?" she said. "Is anyone there? Peet? Marilyn?" No response came. She got up and walked alongside the house, then around the far corner. "Ah, perhaps I've just been out in the sun too long today," she said to herself. "My eyes must be playing tricks on me." She reeled the hose back in place, put it in the shed, and went inside the house to clean up.

CHAPTER FIFTEEN

UNSETTLED HEART

When Peet returned home, he remembered the roots Marilyn had removed for the pond. He walked to the backyard and went to the storage shed to find the large garbage bag filled with native grasses. The bag was hidden in a corner of the shed, behind the tool cart on wheels, and covered by a large tarp. He moved the cart to the side, dragged out the bag, and opened it. The roots were withered and limp, with a brownish hue instead of their natural plum color. He felt frustrated by the lack of control over something he couldn't understand. Sitting on the shed floor, with a hand gripping the side of the bag, he shed a tear, which dropped onto some of the exposed roots.

With that, the grass roots bent forward to face Peet. The roots spoke to him in cracked, faint, and weakened voices. "You have returned, Peet," they said. "We had hoped to meet you. You must ensure the native root metropolis remains intact and strong, so that this grassland biome survives. All the world's other biomes also depend on us grasses here in Barrenville. We cannot reproduce the landscape we once had, as that time has passed, but we can thrive again with the support of the Stewards of Norefole, the Grommels, and now you, Peet. You hold the key to saving both of our worlds. Barrenville must retain its root metropolis for Norefole as well, or its terrain and diversity of life will be no more. The desert sands will devour the other environments within Norefole."

"What do you mean 'both worlds'?" Peet asked.

"The dual heart of the root metropolis of Barrenville and the vase of Norefole have common root threads. Should they splinter, our worlds will be forever altered. The Regal Deer chose you to maintain that balance. Ah, from your presence, we can sense his Juso pumping in your veins. Nearby, our sister roots' whispers grow fainter." Just then, the uprooted roots fell lifeless to the ground.

Peet had so many questions to ask them. "If I'm so powerful, then why couldn't I save these few roots?" he said out loud.

Gromyko discretely approached the storage shed, noticing the open doors. He saw his friend slumped on the cold floor near a large, black bag. Gromyko entered the shed. Peet barely flinched when he noticed Gromyko.

"Are you alright? Did you get injured?" Gromyko asked.

"The roots are dead, Gromyko, and it's all my fault. Look!" Peet said, pointing at the roots on the ground.

Gromyko had already seen death earlier in the day, but seeing the limp roots renewed his sadness. "It is not your fault, my friend," Gromyko said. "Peet, listen to me. The other Grommels are looking for the Cone Witch and her Elicitors. I know she will be searching for you and Marilyn, so I had to come."

"Have you been to the Whimsical Tree?" Peet asked.

"Yes, Peet. The Regal Deer, and all that it brought to this world, is forever lost. We Grommels failed the species—and our mutual worlds," Gromyko stated. "I don't know how the biome will adapt without it." Gromyko's eyes welled up while he tried to comfort Peet.

"I have something to tell you, Gromyko, about the Regal Deer," Peet said. Just then, they heard stirring outside the shed. Gromyko deflated his six sacs to expand his body size, then removed a sliver from his back. Peet quickly picked up the roots and closed the bag. They dashed outside, only to startle Marilyn and send her falling backward into the shrubs along the shed. "Marilyn!" Peet yelled.

"Get me out!" Marilyn demanded. "Who were you talking to? Oh," she said upon seeing Gromyko. After her brother pulled her out of the shrubs, she saw how melancholy he and the Grommel both appeared. "What's wrong?" she inquired.

"Where do I start? The roots you pulled are now officially dead," Peet said. "So is an Ascentia, I mean, the last Regal Deer. Three Genets have been turned into barren trees, and the Witch has returned to Barrenville with Elicitors." Peet poured forth the words rapidly, as if they would hurt less that way. Marilyn began to cry.

"No, no. We'll make things right again," Peet said.

Wanerhess arrived at the Sepvans' home, accompanied by two Clampers.

Hady answered the door. "Wanerhess! Hello. What a nice surprise. Come in."

"Hello, Mrs. Sepvan," Wanerhess said, as the three of them entered the house and followed her into the kitchen.

While they made small talk, Wanerhess peered into the backyard and saw Marilyn, Peet, and Gromyko together. "I see the kids. Why don't you two inquire as to any clamping needs Mrs. Sepvan may have in the near future while I go get the kids. We have some questions for them regarding the pond incident," Wanerhess stated. Hady didn't hesitate, and spoke with the Clampers about the type of shrubbery she wished to add to the backyard.

Wanerhess walked out onto the patio, then through the grasses. The three by the shed looked at him with sadness in their eyes. "I know why you are all sad, but we must consider the consequences if we do nothing," Wanerhess said. "Peet, the Council needs your immediate presence. They are in session now."

"He's right," Gromyko said. "There is a bigger game happening, and we cannot afford to lose sight of it now. Doing so would dishonor the memory of the Regal Deer and many others."

"Gromyko, the van is parked in front," Wanerhess said. "We'll meet you there shortly." Gromyko nodded as the children followed Wanerhess back into the house.

"Mrs. Sepvan, you know the Council has interviewed Jill and Ray regarding the circumstances surrounding the uprooting on your land and the resulting flooding, but the Council has not yet had an opportunity to interview your children," Wanerhess said. "The Council would like to interview Peet next, particularly because of some additional information we have received. He might provide some insight as to the condition of the root metropolis before and after the uprooting. May we have your permission to take him before the Council now?"

"Well, can you have him back before eight?" Hady inquired.

"Of course. I will personally return him home," he responded.

"Peet, can you accompany Mr. Hoise to meet with the Council?" Hady asked.

"Of course, Mom," Peet said.

"Can I go, Mom?" Marilyn asked.

"No, not this time. I need a helper for a new torte recipe," Hady said. "I know you wouldn't want to miss sampling the torte batter, would you?"

"Good luck, Peet," Marilyn said, as she searched for the baking bowls.

"We'll need to ask you a few questions at some point soon too, young lady," Wanerhess said.

"Okay. I'll be here," Marilyn said, now chewing and softening her own rubber spatula, readying it to dip in the batter they would make.

As Peet approached the van, he saw the top of Gromyko's head in the back seat. Peet sat in the last row, facing the back window. With the van heading toward Settlers' Hills, he relaxed in his seat. "I'm sure glad you're here with me, Gromyko," Peet said. Soon the van reached the vicinity of Mera Lab's tower, when they were startled by a sudden, loud noise that came from the side of the van. The Clamper pulled the van over and parked on the side of the road, parallel to the prairie path nearby. Both Clampers in the front of the vehicle got out to inspect the van for any damage. One of the Clampers opened the side door, so they could enjoy the outdoor air.

Gromyko lifted his nose to smell the fresh air, and then immediately yelled out, "Elicitors! Elicitors!" Wanerhess bolted from the second-row seat, through the side door, to call in his Clampers, but they were gone. Peet, strapped in and scared, yelled for Wanerhess. Wanerhess ran to the back of the van to open the back door, which flew upward.

"Ready, Gromyko?" Wanerhess yelled.

"Let's go!" Gromyko exclaimed. Gromyko leapt out at the precise moment Mangar charged the van to snatch Peet. Gromyko, Wanerhess, and the Elicitor all collided with one another, the impact causing them all to fall to the ground. Mangar had been surveying the forest, acting as security for the Witch, when he sensed an intoxicating energy emanating from the van and wrapping around the forest.

Mangar hit the ground backward, with the Grommel on top of him. With the van's back door wide open, the Elicitor's senses became saturated with a foreign, yet enchanting, scent of power, stronger than anything he had experienced before. The power called to him to elicit it.

Gromyko, using his numerous sacs, reconfigured his body to pin the Elicitor to the ground, and even used secretions from his feet to impede the Elicitor's ability to move freely. Gromyko tried several times to use the slivers along his lower back, but he could not detain Mangar and use the slivers simultaneously. Despite all his efforts, the Grommel's tactics weren't enough to trump the head Elicitor, so Gromyko yelled to Wanerhess, "Take Peet away."

Peet was shaking in his seat, watching the full spectrum of events unfold outside the van as if he were watching a three-dimensional movie. Wanerhess ran back to enter the van. Mangar finally released himself from Gromyko's hold then, with great force, threw Gromyko against a nearby tree.

The Elicitor redirected his attention to the van. With his arms stretched in front of him, palms open toward Peet, Mangar readied himself to elicit the boy's powers. "Turn away, Peet. Turn away," Wanerhess yelled as he started the vehicle. Peet was paralyzed, strapped helplessly in his seat. In an instant, Peet felt a chilling sensation, a loud and rapid heart beat, then a rippling sensation moving along his forearms. Peet involuntarily raised his forearms toward the Elicitor. Wanerhess hit the accelerator and, seeing that Peet did not respond to him, swerved the van so that the back door slammed shut. The interference prevented the transfer of energies from Peet to the Elicitor. As they drove off, Mangar ran after them, but was stopped when Gromyko launched a series of slivers at him. Both Peet and Wanerhess witnessed Gromyko leap into the forest and disappear.

A shocked Peet had barely flinched throughout the whole ordeal. He finally tuned into what Wanerhess was saying, which had sounded muffled before. "Peet, the Elicitor now knows," Wanerhess said. "It won't be long before the Cone Witch will also know. Peet! Are you listening?"

"Where are the Clampers?" Peet asked nervously. "We must go back for them."

"I'm afraid we can't stop. It is too late for them," Wanerhess said sadly, as they passed the Clampers' dead bodies on the side of the road. Mangar had thrown them against the pavement from afar. Peet took in a deep, trembling breath as he saw their lifeless forms. "Life that interferes with an Elicitor on this land does not easily walk away unharmed," Wanerhess said. "You were lucky this time, Peet. We had Gromyko." Peet unbuckled his belt and knelt down between the driver and passenger seats, making eye contact with Wanerhess through the van's rearview mirror.

Peet placed his hand on Wanerhess's shoulder while he drove. "What happened back there? What did the Elicitor want from me? Tell me the truth, Wanerhess. What did he do to me?" Peet asked. Peet carefully watched the expression on his friend's face in the mirror. Wanerhess's eyes were full of sorrow and worry.

"We're almost there, Peet," he replied. "The Council will best answer your questions. Please be patient. We are almost there." The van traveled at its fastest speed until they pulled into Settlers' Hills.

When they arrived, two of the Council members, Ruth and John, were waiting outside. "The head Elicitor is just a few miles away, and he knows about Peet," Wanerhess said. "We'll have to prepare, because they will come for him." In a tight cluster, with Peet in the center, they all quickly headed toward Mera Academy.

"Let's get him into the compound," John said, before asking Peet, "Where are your sister and parents?"

"They're at home, but what is going on?" Peet asked.

"Wanerhess, take two Clampers, return to Peet's home, and secure his family's safety," John said. "I'll need you to also bring Marilyn here. Ruth, send additional Clampers to retrieve Ray and Jill. The rest of the Clampers have left to warn the others. Peet, you come with me."

Just as Peet turned to follow John toward the compound, he heard Ruth speak in a foreign, Norefolian tongue. Almost immediately, four hairless, four-legged beasts came through the entrance of Settlers' Hills. They resembled hyenas, but were the size of mountain lions.

"Our Clampers," John explained. "They are also transplants from Norefole."

"I guess they clamp onto more than roots," Peet said with a nervous smile.

"Come along, Peet," John said. "There is no time to waste."

CHAPTER SIXTEEN

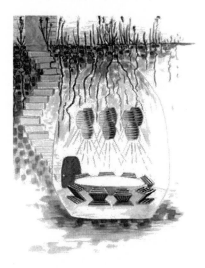

POWERS REVEALED

Peet followed John downstairs into the school library. John turned on the light and walked over to the tallest bookcase against the far wall. He slid his hand over a decorative medallion alongside it, causing the books to rattle. The bookcase sprang open on the side, producing a light from inside. John pulled the bookcase open further, revealing a narrow and long staircase. At the bottom was a glass door that led into an all-glass room, deep in the ground. The single room was twenty feet high, shaped like a slender, octangular capsule with a cone-shaped ceiling and floor. The complex system of long, plum-colored prairie roots draped over much of the room. A series of floating, bee-shaped hives were scattered throughout the room, and provided all its lighting by emitting a blue glow.

Members of the Council were in session reviewing maps of the area when Peet and John entered the room. To Peet, it looked like the hub of a war room. "The head Elicitor knows of Peet's powers," John said. "He tried to elicit them from him on his way here. He did not succeed, thanks to Gromyko and Wanerhess, but we lost two Clampers."

"The Grommels have reported the Regal Deer has passed," Hugh said. "Can you show us the chisel from the Regal Deer, Peet? It was still alive when it was given to you." The Council wanted to study it to learn whether the chisel could be used to counter the impact of the punctures the Witch had made in Barrenville's soil.

"Um..." Peet began, but then paused. "I, um... Well, it is no longer the unique chisel it was, just a simple antler piece."

"What do you mean?" Hugh inquired. Peet explained how the chisel's marrow had seeped into his skin, and how the chisel became lighter in weight and shed its bark.

Peet removed the antler from his pocket and placed it on the table. The full Council was captivated by his explanation and at a loss for words—a rare thing. Now that the Council had learned that Peet had the Regal Deer's Juso, keeping him hidden from the Elicitors and the Witch would be its greatest challenge yet.

"This has never happened before!" John exclaimed. "And from the most powerful Ascentia of a biome, for that matter."

"A creature will never pass through life without creating

ripples in the universal matrix of energy, and apparently the Regal Deer was not done here," Hugh said. "The Regal Deer was not destined to survive on a collapsed cliff, or to serve as a home for the Genets. No, Peet. The Regal Deer had an unparalleled ability to heal, repair, and vitalize grassland roots. It was alone in this task when it finally came to rest in Barrenville. Peet, its final contribution was bestowing its Juso upon you. It continues to live through you. However, Ascentia Juso attracts Elicitors, so you have become even more desirable to the Elicitors and the Witch." Peet looked at him with wide eyes, while clutching the edge of the table.

"Through your Steward training and your exposure to the Clade powers, you have mastered certain essential skills," Hugh said. "Based on your encounter with the head Elicitor, you must know; he would not have tried to elicit you otherwise. Mangar himself would have been confused by the duality of your powers. Peet, you must realize your ancestral powers now."

Peet observed the Council carefully, beginning to understand for the first time what they saw in him. He had flashbacks of events from even before his first encounter with the Regal Deer. For as long as he could remember, he had relished seeking shapes and figures in busy textures. He found great joy in spending time in Barrenville's prairie, as he could always see beyond the endless, multicolored landscape and use its patterns and shapes to find the rare barren spots. The eco-jars were souvenirs of these visuals. Peet recalled that his Steward had him painting only in long, vertical and horizontal strokes, brushing across the full canvas.

Then he would simply trace what he saw within the canvas, and images would magically reveal themselves. He recalled how, in Norefole, he felt his best when he stood among the Imajs.

Peet gasped. "I'm an Imaj!" he said in a near whisper.

Peet found himself noticing that the blue hives providing the lighting above did not exist as random stand-alone hives, but now formed a connected structure. Sometime during the meeting, the hives had sunk close to the conference table and arranged themselves into a pattern, which Peet noticed looked like a model plane looming in the air. With more careful observation, he saw that this plane-like structure had a floss-thin seal with a glimmering coating around it. He approached it and placed his hand on its far side, causing the entire image to loosen. As he had seen the Imajs do, he then slightly retracted his hand while he concentrated on the image. He next tapped the image and extracted the model plane. "I'm an Imaj," he whispered again to himself as he examined it.

"Yes, Peet. Your ancestors were of the Imaj Clade," Hugh said. He was surprised to see that, unlike the Norefolian Imajs, Peet did not require a hard surface in which to find an image. With this awesome revelation, Peet felt goose bumps throughout his body. "Humans can draw from the same ancient sources of power as the Clades," Hugh continued. "Humans once used their ancestral powers but, after just a few recent generations ceased to do so, they caused the powers to hibernate."

"But why would we have stopped using them?" Peet asked.

"Humans stopped using their powers for the same reason

they plunder their own environment," Hugh responded. "They forgot what was important."

"Where do these powers come from?" Peet asked.

"Our shared universe has many places that have evolved differently, for example, the Earth world and the Norefole world," Reid said. "In both worlds, Norefolians and humans alike hold our planet's shapes in our eyes, a sign of our connectedness to a single universe. Since our pace of evolution and environment differs, we might look different from you, but the residue of our common, universal energies exists in your fibers, as in ours. Our worlds merely tracked down different veins of the same organism in the ever-expanding universe. So you see, we are not that different from you after all."

"Clade powers remain ancient in their truest and raw form and have been kept continuously alive, resulting in the evolution of the Five Clades and interrelated societies, such as us Stewards," John said.

"Yet through exposure to the various Clade powers, humans can begin to discover their own lineage," Hugh said. "Marilyn found it easy to access her power because she demanded it and the conditions were ripe. Luckily, she was able to produce a semblance of her undeveloped power in time to protect herself at the battle of the Five Clades Garden. Peet, your discovery of your own powers was hindered in Norefole because you carried the chisel, which had magical marrow and dominated your hibernating Clade power. Jill is an Ara. If you recall, she was twice positioned behind the revolving bands, as an Ara cannot enclose another Ara. On the other hand, she was never interested in the possibility of having a power; she remains indifferent and detached from that possibility."

"What about Ray? What power does he have?" Peet asked.

"Yes, Ray also has Clade abilities," John said. "The King has ordered a unique regimen for his training, however."

"Could he be an Elicitor?" Peet asked.

"He is capable of having the characteristics of any of the Five Clades," John said. "Regardless, he will have a different perspective through the Stewards' training."

Just then, the door flung open and in walked Ruth with Marilyn, Jill, and Ray. They were thrilled to see Peet. Jill yelled his name as she ran over to hug him. "We heard a couple of Clampers were killed and that you were in the same car," Jill said.

"It's okay, Jill. I'm alright," he said.

Jill leaned in and whispered to Peet, "Does this have to do with what you told me at recess?"

"Yes, but we're going to be alright," Peet said. "I understand now." As the words flowed from Peet's lips, he heard himself speaking in a stronger, more confident voice.

Although Ray had never witnessed Clade powers, he sensed an unusual and unexplainable shift in energy within himself since his encounter with the Elicitor, as if it had triggered a memory. "What are we doing here?" Ray asked in a whisper, looking around the room. The style and contents of the room reminded him of Norefole. He missed Norefole's unusual architecture and the altruistic, tight-knit community he longed for in his world.

179

Marilyn's attention was fixed on the roots that cloaked much of the glass. She paced back and forth across the room, looking at the variations of root shapes and sizes.

Gromyko was the last to join them. He had been severely injured by Mangar, and his skin had tears and bruises. He reported that all the Grommels and several Clampers were stationed at each corner of Mera Academy, and that any of them could smell an Elicitor's presence from afar.

"It's time!" Ruth announced. "We have not confirmed how many Elicitors are here, but we have eight Grommels, the full Council of twelve Stewards, and an entourage of Clampers ready to fight to protect the root metropolis. We also need to find them a safe place here within the compound," she continued, pointing at the children. Hugh and John, sitting opposite the entrance, walked toward Ruth.

"Peet, Mom is making strawberry torte for desert tonight," Marilyn whispered to Peet. Jill, who was standing near Peet, smiled when she overheard Marilyn's comment.

"Shhh..." Peet responded with a half smile, knowing his little sister did not truly understand the seriousness of their predicament. Apparently, neither did his salivating mouth. Ray joined Ruth, John, and Hugh.

"Are we in trouble?" Ray asked Ruth in a cautious voice. Ruth looked at Hugh, who nodded to her.

"You are not in danger, Ray, but they are," Ruth said, pointing at Peet, Marilyn, and Jill. "The Elicitors want to steal their powers."

"We don't have time to explain now, but understand they are more vulnerable to an Elicitor than the rest of us, including you," John said sternly. "You must help us protect them from the Elicitors and the Cone Witch."

"She's here?" Ray asked, somewhat worriedly. He had been transformed by the Witch before, and wondered whether she would want to do it again.

Ray listened carefully, but felt confused about these purported powers of theirs. "Even if they had powers, how could someone take them away, and why?" he wondered. Nonetheless, he felt a strong duty to protect his friends, as they were as close to him as siblings. Ray turned to observe Peet and the girls. They all appeared vulnerable and feeble to him. Peet was wiping his allergy-inflamed nose, Marilyn had her two hands and tiny body pressed against the glass, and Jill was cleaning her eyeglasses to better see the roots. "I'm faster and stronger than those three, so I can definitely help," Ray said in a dominating voice. Ray now felt like warrior material, ready for combat. The Norefolians had asked him to be part of their defense team to protect his friends and his hometown, and he wasn't about to let them down. Besides, the Elicitor he met earlier didn't scare him.

After numerous instructions and warnings, the children were led out of the capsule room, back through the library, and into one of the classrooms. "Ray, while we prepare to fight, you and two Stewards will stay behind for their protection like we talked about," Hugh said, pointing at Peet, Marilyn, and Jill. "The Stewards will inform you about these powers you keep hearing about. They will help you understand."

CHAPTER SEVENTEEN

THE FINAL STAND

Mangar retreated to the cave and notified the Cone Witch of Peet's extraordinary and unusual blend of powers—something beyond that of a Clade. He also reported about the bark shavings found on the upper cliff above the Whimsical Tree's plateau, and showed her the bark. It had familiar etching on it. "Of course! I don't know why I didn't see this before," the Witch said. A hopeful expression returned to her pale face. "Give me those bark shavings so I can make tea. They should still have the residue of the Regal Deer, and the tea will counter the effects of the toxins that chisel left in me earlier. Then we can focus on capturing the new Ascentia—that boy." Mangar nodded, as he had reached the same conclusion. He split open a rotting log he spotted in the cave and promptly started a fire.

"We will first create a battle of roots beneath the ground, then focus on creating a battle above ground," the Witch said. "Dropping cone seedlings all across the forest floor will also create a distraction for our friends, buying us time to find this boy. Once my cone seedlings are fertilized, they will uncoil deep into the fertile ground of Barrenville. The seedlings will then do as their ancestors did before them. They'll plunge deep and wide into the earth, exuding all of their destructive ancestral traits. In time, my seedlings will take all the nutrients, leaving the root metropolis to starve."

"Ingenious as always," Mangar said, prodding the fire.

"How are we doing with reinforcements?" the Witch asked.

"The next army of Elicitors should find us soon. They will have our traditional weapons to deal with the Stewards and their allies. Whether they left Grommel Lake with their new powers or not, I'm certain they got on the aerial bridges. Without the porters, however, they could be anywhere. Perhaps we should have directed more of the army to Grommel Lake straight after leaving the Kingdom." He paused for a while in reflection, then smiled. "I'm certain those Grommels back home never saw us coming. How could they? There were too many of us with powers."

"Yet, you lost your army to the Grommels here," the Witch said.

"In this world, your Highness, the Grommels have an

advantage over us. Back home, their spray of slivers can only prick our skin and stop the transfer of powers. Here, they can kill us."

"I see," she responded, while sipping her tree bark tea from a wooden remnant.

After the Witch had her tea, she got up without a struggle for the first time since her arrival in Barrenville. She walked outside the cave to take in the view, with Mangar following. "You are ready then?" Mangar asked.

"Yes," she said, feeling renewed. "I feel my strength quickly returning to me."

They walked south through the center of the forest toward Settlers' Hills. "The Stewards have had time to develop all the grounds here," she said, noting the vastness and complexity of the area. "We know how they like labyrinths. We will have to wait until they surface. When our reinforcements come, station at least one of them overlooking the entrance to their compound."

The Witch then found the spot where she desired to nest. She looked out long into the forest— the textures, the density of objects, the distances between things. Her perspective of the forest was like that of a fisherman looking out to sea, feeling the depth of life all around her and yearning to plunge in and interfere with that life. She walked to a clearing, where she bent down to her knees and tucked her legs underneath her cone dress.

"Here I shall rest. You may leave me now," she told Mangar. She nestled into the ground, her upper body rigidly straight and her stick arms resting alongside her body. Mangar stayed near for a while to ensure she was alone.

With the base of the Witch's full cone dress touching the ground, many of the flaps on it opened, and a dozen cone seedlings sprang forth. They rolled from her cone dress and encircled her. This ring of seedlings was her sensor, as well as her anchor to the ground beneath. A growing population of her own species could hijack the heart of one of Earth's biomes.

"Go, my seedlings. Expand this spine of forest within Barrenville and deplete the pools of grasses—the natives to the west and the hybrids to the east," the Witch said. As she meditated, she harnessed her energies. Mangar then perceived his Elicitors arriving and went to meet them, leaving the entranced Witch alone.

At the same time, the Grommels, Clampers, and Stewards prepared to leave Mera Academy and comb the grounds for the Elicitors and the Cone Witch. Wanerhess explained the Witch's nesting behavior and where in the forest she would most likely be found. John trekked ahead of the group as a scout. The other Stewards gathered their traditional Norefolian weapons. Each spear was retractable, with various-sized splinter spears branching off. Stewards were masterful at handling such weapons, all of which had reflective gems embedded on both sides for control over pulling or pushing of energies, and which could cause momentary blindness. These weapons mirrored the reflecting qualities of the Grommels' eyes and the versatility of their sacs.

The Witch's cone seedlings gravitated to the eastern and western borders of the forest. The air cooled gradually, allowing her seedlings to drill and penetrate deep into the ground. Like teeth, the cones' roots tore, pinched, and prickled the surrounding flora. The Witch was proud of her contamination blending into the forest. One of the cone seedlings, which had not yet migrated or embedded itself in the ground, began to rattle loudly, waking the Witch from her meditation. She flung her arms forward, causing her body to tilt forward and the back of her cone shell to rise slightly off the ground. Nearby, she saw a Steward lurking. She untucked her legs from beneath her cone, like a beetle would under its shell.

On her brittle knees, the Witch moved out of the clearing and closer to the trees, so that she could appear as a shadow until she closed in on the Steward. She stayed as still as a tree, her overall form blending into the forest. John unknowingly walked near the Witch. When he was within her reach, she opened her eyes and slowly uncoiled directly behind him.

As the Witch stood up, Wanerhess catapulted himself at her from the side, knocking her across the forest floor. When she landed, she dislocated one arm and one leg, but quickly snapped them back into place. "You Norefolian fools!" she yelled. The air chilled as her face tightened into an aggressive expression. She raised her eyebrows high and grinned insidiously.

Between her bark tea, her meditation efforts, and her seedlings reaching the native roots, the Witch had greatly counteracted the effects of the chisel and nearly regained her full strength. She leaped toward John, who was frozen from shock, and quickly transformed him into a barren tree. She briskly removed two handfuls of sharp scales from her outer shell and whipped them at Wanerhess. Surprisingly limber and quick for his age, Wanerhess dropped to the ground like a crouching tiger, and the scales caught on the trees behind him. The Witch weakened again, as she'd used too much of her energy too soon. The air became warmer again.

Wanerhess discretely took out his retractable, three-part Norefolian spear, lined with blue sapphires. He hid it along his side. As the Witch plucked out another set of scales, Wanerhess charged again, hoping to reach her before she could throw her scales a second time. Her arm stiffened, however, as she waited for him to get closer. He then revealed his Norefolian weapon and, with the quick movement of one lever, turned it into a fully extended spear. The Witch was momentarily blinded by its blue jewels, but she threw the scales in his general direction, hitting Wanerhess repeatedly. The sharp scales cut like glass. He was relentless, however, and his charge continued. She moved at an angle to get out of his path, but his spear slit her side. The injury caused her cone shell to shatter, and she fell to her knees.

Wanerhess walked around her from behind, now using the spear as a staff. He knew he had to exterminate the aggressor species. In one fell swoop, he smashed the staff into the Witch's vertebrae. She collapsed to the ground. She now lay on her side, with one arm stretched above her head. As she drew her last breath, she pivoted to face the treetops and the sky. Wanerhess looked back at the lifeless Witch on the ground—a smooth, cone-shaped lump with branch-like limbs.

Meanwhile, the full troop of Grommels, a pack of Clampers and several Stewards searched for the Elicitors and the Witch. Together, they stood a chance of defeating them. Elicitors were on foreign land—never before had they touched Barrenville soil—making them more vulnerable to attack.

The two sides faced off in the fields alongside the forest. Now, they would battle on Earth's turf. Both sides lined up in rows like pieces on a chess board. Eight Grommels expanded to their full size, ten Clampers transformed into four-legged beasts, and nine armed Stewards aligned themselves against the small but fierce Elicitor army, few of whom still carried other Clade powers. Each side charged across the sloped terrain. In long leaps, the Grommels zigzagged down the terrain opposite the Elicitors, with the Stewards and Clampers running directly behind them.

As the charge began, the same swarm of birds that had visited the Sepvans' home now cut between the opposing sides like an endless, flowing river that could not be crossed. The birds flew so close together, and they were so numerous, that they formed an impenetrable wall of flapping wings that was also deafening. The two battling sides ceased their charge, but the fight still appeared inevitable. Gromyko, weighing the odds of battle against his fear for the children's safety, nodded to the Grommel second in command, who took over. Gromyko left the troop and headed back to Mera Academy. Gromyko calculated it could be hours before the wall of birds left, and the children were his highest priority. In leaps and bounds, he achieved an unsurpassed speed as he headed toward the school.

Back at Mera Academy, Peet reflected on the uniqueness of his dual powers, although he did not yet have full control of them. He also had a very vivid picture of the Norefolians battling, and he longed to help. He felt he could no longer be quarantined in the classroom.

"Where are you going, Peet?" Marilyn asked as he quietly headed toward the door. Everyone in the room turned to look at him.

"I'm just going to the restroom," Peet said. One of the Stewards got up to escort him.

"No. It won't be necessary," Peet replied. "I'll be back shortly." Rather than head to the restroom, however, he walked briskly through the exit doors and headed to Six-Pine Alley, his favorite spot in Settlers' Hills. "I couldn't be in there another moment," he said out loud, wiping his sweaty forehead from all the anxiety. "Besides, I have a better hiding place."

When Peet arrived, he brushed his hands against the trees to release their natural pine scent, which he always found calming. All was quiet around him. Between two of the pines on the same side was a well-used, needle-free resting place Peet had created. At recess, he often played there, visualizing images on the ground and on the bark of the trees. The spot was surrounded by thick and heavy pine branches, muffling much of the noise made by the other kids.

"I'm an Imaj with Juso," Peet said, understanding why he could spend endless hours finding images in objects. Now he knew he had found his ancestral power, and he could access it.

Suddenly, he felt a tingling sensation along his arms.

An Elicitor, who was keeping watch for any movement at the compound, had spied Peet moving through the pines. The Elicitor stood at the entrance to Six-Pine Alley and began to elicit Peet, who instinctively extended his arms toward the Elicitor. Gromyko, who was returning to the compound, immediately recognized that someone was being elicited. Gromyko quickly jumped into midair, drawing closer to the Elicitor while throwing slivers at him. Next, he leapt on top of him, jabbing the slivers into the Elicitor and killing him instantly.

*　　*　　*

The birds finally descended, and the battle ensued. The armed Stewards, Grommels, and Clampers charged. With their weapons drawn, the Elicitors rushed toward their opponents while maintaining their row. The Elicitors' staffs fanned out into several spears of different sizes, similar to but less ornate than the Stewards' weaponry. The Grommels, once close enough to the Elicitors, leapt into the air to throw their arrow-like slivers. The Elicitors broke formation to avoid the air attack, while also thwarting the slivers by fanning their weapons. One Elicitor speared a Grommel as he readied to leap on him. Although the Elicitors were greatly outnumbered, they were powerful and sophisticated in the art of war, each able to fight five attackers at once.

The Clampers, more powerful than bulls, charged the

Elicitors next. The Elicitors were able to use their weapons' length to prevent the beasts from reaching them. Their proximity to one another, however, allowed the Elicitors to rope the Clampers' legs with onyx fiber, preventing movement without severing their limbs. Soon all the beasts were on the ground and hogtied.

When the Stewards caught up, a thunderous clash of weapons echoed and vibrated into the nearby forest. While Stewards fought with weapons, Grommels wrestled with the Elicitors. Elicitors continued to fiercely fan their weapons and jab their opponents. One Elicitor held two Stewards at once with his bare hands and smashed them together, killing them instantly. Two Elicitors, who fell to the ground injured, were then ripped apart by the tied-up beasts nearby. Other Grommels continued to hurl slivers at the Elicitors.

The combined allies were relentless in their attack against the Elicitors, until only two remained. Mangar and the other remaining Elicitor then saw an unprecedented pack of beasts on the western horizon. The pack galloped toward them with a uniform guttural sound that signaled victory. The Elicitors ran into the forest in the hopes of losing the herd of beasts. The Stewards immediately tended to the roped beasts who, once freed, joined the pack.

In the cover of night, Mangar and one other surviving Elicitor finally reached the area where he had left the Witch to meditate. They found her lifeless and deformed body on the forest floor. The Elicitors had lost the war, along with their hopes of obtaining permanent powers. No longer part of the Kingdom and now without the Witch, they would continue to starve for other Clade powers. Only two Elicitors made their way to the torrent, where the aerial bridge had delivered them earlier, and escaped Earth back to Norefole.

*   *   *

"How did you know to find me?" Peet asked as he and Gromyko both headed to the classroom.

"I don't know," Gromyko said. "We have this strange connection and, just as before, I felt it calling."

Gromyko stayed with the four children and two Stewards until the others returned. Once the group was reunited, Wanerhess gathered Gromyko, Peet, and three Stewards, and led them to the barren tree where John was encapsulated. Once there, the Stewards guided Peet on how to find the image of John within the tree and how to extract him. Peet tilted his head and focused on the image, until he saw the glittering outline. Peet successfully loosened and extracted John's image from the tree. The others quickly grabbed John, who was still asleep. Wanerhess shook him and called his name. "What happened? Wait! Wanerhess?" asked John, seeing his friend standing over him and remembering their encounter with the Witch.

"We have a hybrid production to harvest soon, so no time for naps," Wanerhess said to John.

"Where is she?" John asked, exasperated. The Stewards and Wanerhess described the demise of the Witch and their battle with the Elicitor army. John shook his head, disappointed he had missed the fight.

"I had that creature exactly where I wanted until you interfered," John said jokingly, looking at Wanerhess.

"Sure you did," Wanerhess said.

The group pushed onward in search of the Genets. Peet examined hundreds of trees along the way to the double cliff, until he saw the distinct images of the Genets in three different trees. Peet ran to them yelling, "No! No! No!" Peet tried to extract Sal, Jacq, and David from the trees, but it was too late. One of the Stewards then made a guttural sound that called for all nearby Clampers. Peet was more surprised by the calling than by the presence of the beasts. The Clampers carefully removed each of the small Genet trees by their roots, as well as what was left of the Whimsical Tree, and prepared burial sites for the deceased along the outskirts of Settlers' Hills near the lake.

Other Clampers combed the forest for cone seedlings, surgically plucking out each one they found. Peet and Hugh closely followed Wanerhess and the line of Clampers. Along the way, Hugh taught Peet how to access and utilize his unique Ascentia energies. Each time the Clampers removed a seedling, Peet held his hand over the wound to repair and heal the land. Peet experienced the gusher of wisps for the first time, and then repeatedly with each wound he repaired.

Upon completing this process, seven Grommels, ten Stewards, numerous Clampers, and the four children gathered to attend a burial service conducted by Wanerhess. Although

Stewards, a Grommel, Clades, and an Ascentia had been lost, two worlds were saved.

"Wanerhess," Peet whispered. "Jacq, David, and Sal weren't the Genets' true Norefolian names, were they?"

"No, they pulled those names from the books they read," Wanerhess said.

"Well, they fit them," Peet responded, with tears in his eyes.

At the ceremony's end, Wanerhess drove the children home late that night. All four of them were quiet most of the ride home.

"Could a Cone Witch or an Elicitor ever return to Barrenville?" Marilyn asked Wanerhess.

"We removed all of the Cone Witch's seedlings," he replied. "Luckily, they never germinated, and the damaged roots were quickly repaired. As for the Elicitors, I'm quite certain they won't want to return to our hometown again."

"Those Elicitors never frightened me anyway," Ray said, before he closed the van door and began to walk up his driveway.

"Bye," they all responded.

When they arrived at Jill's house, she said, "I guess I'll see you guys back at school. Perhaps, now I'll get to see what happens at the recreation center. I'm more interested in that now." She winked at Marilyn, then closed the van door.

Finally, they arrived at the Sepvans' house. As the three of them approached the doorway, Hady answered. "I'm sorry we are so late, Mrs. Sepvan," Wanerhess said. "They did well, but the meeting went longer than expected. Everything is cleared up now." Hady was quite forgiving when she saw her children's tired faces. Before Wanerhess got into the van, he turned back toward the front door, where Peet and Marilyn were waving at the window. He smiled and winked back at them.

"Let's go visit Mom and Dad," Marilyn said.

"That's a good idea," Peet said.

Hady had returned to the kitchen table, where she and Ansel were reviewing paperwork. "Tired, Mom," Marilyn said, as she placed her arms around her mother's neck.

"Yes, I can see," Hady said.

"Why don't you guys go get ready for bed?" Hady said. "We'll talk tomorrow morning about how your day went."

"Goodnight," Marilyn and Peet said as they headed toward their bedrooms.

When Peet was in his room, he picked up his baseball mitt from the chest and put back the antler. This act had become as routine as brushing his teeth before bed. He paused and removed the antler again, gripping it over his heart. "Thank you for choosing me to help save our grasslands," Peet said. He felt privileged and humbled to be part of the Regal Deer's legacy.

*   *   *

Six months later, the Council met with Wanerhess and Peet in the Mera Lab conference room. "With this last output of hybrid grasses, I'd like to report we are officially more than seventy percent hybrid across the continent," Wanerhess said.

"I've cataloged the spots where I found some small overgrowth bundles in the root metropolis," said Peet, who now seemed five years more mature in his demeanor. He folded the town map he once used for eco-jars into his pocket. "I'll be tending to those spots throughout the next month, but we have no more oddities in the grasses."

"That means Barrenville's native grasses and the dual-heart valve of the root metropolis are finally secure after all these years," Hugh said.

"Indeed. Our once-fractured grassland biome has been restored, and our mission fulfilled," Ruth said.

"Well, that really depends on how you define fractured," Reid said. They continued to plan to debate, then debate to plan, as was the Council way.

*   *   *

Back at the Kingdom, the heads of the Four Clades and the King visited Grommel Lake. They found the Grommels busy sifting the lake waters and shoveling sand away. While Grog spoke to the King, Grayle and other Grommels standing nearest the vase began cheering and leaping in the air.

"What could all that commotion be about?" asked the King, half smiling.

Grog noted from across the lake that one of those cheering and leaping was his daughter. "Well, she would have reason to get commotional, I hope," Grog said, embarrassed. Grog then felt a sensation on his hands and feet. He saw the spots on his skin were gone and the webbing stronger.

"Ah, a good father you are," the King replied, noticing Grog examining his hands and feet.

Word quickly spread across the lake that the vase had suddenly shed its red-tainted threading and all of its imperfections. The vase was lustrous and smooth once again.

Norefole would thrive.

The End

CPSIA information can be obtained at www.ICGtesting.com
Printed in the USA
LVOW12s2017170414

382180LV00002B/6/P